KT-389-822

# MAX

## The
## DETECTIVE CAT

# The
# DISAPPEARING
# DIVA

illustrated by
**NICOLA KINNEAR**

*Sarah Todd Taylor*

nosy
crow

First published 2018 by Nosy Crow Ltd
The Crow's Nest, 14 Baden Place, Crosby Row
London SE1 1YW
www.nosycrow.com

ISBN: 978 1 78800 035 2

Nosy Crow and associated logos are trademarks
and/or registered trademarks of Nosy Crow Ltd

Text copyright © Sarah Todd Taylor, 2018
Illustrations © Nicola Kinnear, 2018

The right of Sarah Todd Taylor and Nicola Kinnear to be identified as the
author and illustrator respectively has been asserted.

All rights reserved

This book is sold subject to the condition that it shall not,
by way of trade or otherwise, be lent, hired out or otherwise circulated in
any form of binding or cover other than that in which it is published.
No part of this publication may be reproduced, stored in a retrieval
system, or transmitted in any form or by any means
(electronic, mechanical, photocopying, recording or otherwise)
without the prior written permission of Nosy Crow Ltd.

A CIP catalogue record for this book will be available from the British Library

Printed and bound in the UK by Clays Ltd, St Ives Plc

Papers used by Nosy Crow are made from wood grown in
sustainable forests.

3 5 7 9 10 8 6 4 2

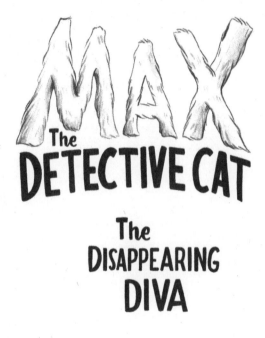

# MAX
## The
## DETECTIVE CAT

### The
### DISAPPEARING
### DIVA

ST. HELENS LIBRARIES

3 8055 35039 6297

| St Helens Council Schools Library Service | |
| --- | --- |
| 3805535039629 | |
| PETERS | 10-Dec-2018 |
| JF | £6.99 |
| | |

*For Cat*

S. T.

*For my mum and dad*

N. K.

# CHAPTER 1
## The Rooftops of London

Maximilian peered through the basket at the oily river and wrinkled his powdered nose. The smell of the city was harsh and sour, and everywhere seemed to be made of noise. He was not used to this.

Maximilian was used to silver dishes, velvet cushions and the very finest salmon soufflé. Maximilian was used to his beloved Countess Arlington fussing over him at least six times a day and eight times on Saturdays. Maximilian was *not* used to being stuffed into a smelly cat basket and sent off with one of the maids late at night and without so much as a sniff of his supper.

The maid in question, a rather clumsy girl with rosy cheeks, pressed her face to the basket. Maximilian fixed her with what he hoped was a regal stare and miaowed his "a terrible mistake has been made, take me back home at once" miaow.

The girl made little shushing noises. "Don't worry, you silly scrap," she whispered. "I'm not really going to drown you, no matter what she says."

Maximilian frowned. He didn't know what drowning was, but the way the girl said it made him think it wasn't something nice like salmon mousse or tummy tickles. He could not think why the silly child had brought him out on such a cold, damp night to sit by a smelly river. Countess Arlington would be worrying about him by now. Maximilian started to scratch at the basket, taking care not to snag any of his beautiful fur.

The girl looked out over the river. "I don't know quite what I'm going to do with you though," she said. "And I have to go back soon."

Maximilian let out a low, rather ungentlemanly growl and lay down with his chin on his paws. It was rude to growl, but the girl was being extremely stupid. Everyone, in fact, had been behaving rather stupidly today, ever since his little adventure with the soil and the mouse and the maid.

Maximilian lived in Arlington Grove, the most fashionable townhouse in London. To be precise, Maximilian lived on a red velvet cushion in the drawing room of Arlington Grove, the most fashionable townhouse in London. His cushion was set into the window seat to catch the afternoon sun and was extremely comfortable, but he had never seen the rest of the house.

Until this morning.

This morning the maid had left the drawing-room door ajar after changing the pink roses in the vases and Maximilian had followed her out and explored. He found a spider in a plant pot and pounced on it, scattering soil across the cream carpets. He left muddy footprints on the crisp white bed sheets in the guest rooms. He scampered down a long staircase to the kitchens, where he had great fun chasing some mice till one ran into the middle of the room and a maid holding a pan full of fat screamed and dropped it all over him.

Maximilian was quickly returned to the drawing room, covered in soil and dripping with greasy fat. Countess Arlington took one look at him, shrieked and ordered him to be washed with disinfecting soap that stung his eyes and got into his nose and ears. Clean and dry, he was put back on his cushion to sit quietly while the maids fussed around, clearing up the mess he had made.

Later on, the butler had stuffed him into the cat basket and the maid had brought him down to the river.

Maximilian stared at the girl, who was looking from side to side as if deciding what to do. He was getting colder and damper and had had rather enough of being cried at. It was time to take matters into his own paws. Somewhere out in the city was his home and Countess Arlington, and Maximilian wanted to be in that somewhere, not trapped in a basket by a smelly river. The cat basket was held shut by a small bar threaded through two loops on the front. Maximilian squeezed a paw through the latticed willow of the basket, wincing as a sharp piece of wood scratched the soft pad on his paw. After a little wiggling he managed to get close to the bar. He gave it a little tap and, as it clattered to the ground, sprang at the basket's lid. It flew open and he leapt out. He heard a gasp behind him, but there was no time to lose and, ignoring the girl's cries of "Come back, you silly puss!" Maximilian fled as fast as he could out into the night.

The city at night was a very different place from one cushioned and perfumed room. For one thing, there seemed to be feet everywhere. Rough, booted feet that kicked out at him, hobnailed clogs that threatened to crush his tail, daintily shod feet in T-bar shoes that stepped quickly away in alarm as he dashed past. The streets were packed to bursting. Maximilian could not believe how noisy the world was. Sounds came at him from every direction, and all of them were loud and harsh and not at all welcoming to a cat on his own for the first time in his life.

He ran till his paws were red and sore, and then he looked for a place to hide and rest. The city was a most confusing place. Whichever way he went seemed to lead back to the river, a great expanse of water that glistened in the moonlight and smelled like. . . Maximilian tried to think of what it smelled like, but his whole life he had been surrounded by perfume and talcum and dried pieces of flower called potpourri. The only smell he knew he didn't like was flea powder and even *that* smelled better than this. It was a smell that had something fishy in it, but not the sort of fish that Maximilian thought he would want to eat.

Maximilian decided to ignore the fact that his tummy was feeling empty. There was a bridge a little way ahead of him where a cat might, if a cat were lucky, find somewhere soft to lie down. He was tired and had missed at least two of his daily catnaps, so it was time to catch up.

More important even than a catnap, it was time for one of his tail grooms. Maximilian was a beautiful cat, but he was particularly proud of his tail. It was long and white and gloriously fluffy. Countess Arlington said that it was like a feather duster (not that she had ever had cause to *use* a feather duster). She called Maximilian "my fluffy angel", which he loved. Having such a magnificent tail does not come by luck or accident, however, and it was sheer hard work, and eight grooms a day, that kept Maximilian's looking so wonderful. He sneaked a look back at it. It was a little bedraggled and grubby on account of the damp puddles he had run through, and he was going to have to give it particular attention to bring it up to his usual standard.

There was nothing soft to lie down on under the bridge, only hard brickwork and dust that made Maximilian shudder with dismay. How he wished that he was back on his comfy window cushion, with the soft velvet pile that lay in just the right direction for his fur. He padded around, testing the ground with a paw to see if there was anywhere that was clean.

"Well, pick a place and be quick about it," said a voice somewhere in the dark. "Some of us have been hunting all day."

Maximilian froze. The maids at Arlington Grove had been very fond of telling him he was spoiled and that out in what they called "the real world" cats were not treated as well as he was. One rather spiteful girl in particular would delight in holding him up to the window to point out stray cats in the street below. They looked scruffy and ill cared for with their scraggy tails and matted fur. "Proper cats, that's what they are. Not pampered balls of fluff. They'd make mincemeat of you, my lad," the girl would say, shaking Maximilian so roughly that his fur would feel quite out of sorts. What if this were one of those strays, come to make mincemeat of him?

"I put that a little bluntly," said the voice. "There's plenty of space, but I'm really very tired." From the shadows at the edge of the bridge there emerged a sleek black cat. It had one startlingly green eye and both of its ears were torn, but its coat was glossy and well kept and it moved with elegance and poise.

"I'm sorry," Maximilian said, relaxing enough to remember his manners. "Am I trespassing?"

The black cat cocked its head to the side and studied Maximilian with its one eye. Maximilian began to feel rather self-conscious. He pulled his tummy in and tried to stand up a little straighter. Eventually the cat said, "You're a little on the posh side for this part of town."

Maximilian nodded. "I'm just . . . visiting," he said.

"Hungry?" asked the cat.

Maximilian was about to say "no", but before he could, his tummy let out a groan that most emphatically meant "yes". The black cat smiled and fetched something small and furry from a mound in the corner. "Mouse," it said. "Quite fresh."

"I've never had mouse," Maximilian said, nosing the furry scrap.

The black cat nodded. "I suppose you're one of those big city cats who only eat the best salmon. How did you end up here?"

In between tasty morsels of mouse (such a delicious meal) Maximilian told the black cat all about Arlington Grove, and about life with his beloved Countess, and how much she would be missing him. Maximilian told the cat about the Countess's dinner parties and the concerts she would host in the drawing room of Arlington Grove and about how she liked to hold cocktail parties where her elegantly dressed friends stood around the grand piano singing songs from musicals and making the sound that he made when someone stood on his tail.

The black cat's one good eye narrowed a little. "It sounds like a very comfortable life," he said, "if a little . . . small."

Maximilian bristled. Life with the Countess had been wonderful. What would a stray alley cat know anyway?

"One room was never enough for me," the black cat said. "A cat needs space to feel alive."

"One room was plenty for me," Maximilian said, ignoring how much fun it had been to scamper through the corridors of Arlington Grove and how disappointed he had been when the butler caught him. "There was always plenty to see from the window, more than you could ever imagine."

At this the black cat raised an eyebrow. "Really?" he said. "I wonder. Can you climb?"

An hour later they were on the rooftops. Maximilian had marvelled at the deftness with which the black cat (whose name was Oscar) scaled the buildings, leaping across window sills and turning in mid-air to catch the edge of a drainpipe. Maximilian had followed slowly, opting for the safety of fire-escape staircases and needing to be coaxed into jumping from one rooftop to another.

"Are you a cat or a human?" Oscar said at the fifth jump. "Hurry up. We're almost there."

Maximilian glared at him. He did not like being laughed at and he was sure that all these acrobatics had made his fur scruffy. What *must* his glorious fluffy tail look like? He paused at the edge of a rooftop and examined it for dirt smudges. "Almost where?" he said irritably.

"You'll see," said Oscar, flipping himself backwards over the edge and landing on the guttering of the roof opposite. He disappeared over the top of the curved roof and from the other side Maximilian heard his voice call out, "You're going to miss it if you don't hurry up!"

Maximilian followed carefully, trying not to slip on the tiles. At the top he paused.

Beneath him, the great city spread like a carpet of lights twinkling in the darkness. Up on the rooftops it was quieter. The noise of the streets softened and blurred into a gentle hum. Above them the moonlight glowed behind the clouds, picking out their billowing shapes in the inky purple sky.

"Lovely, isn't it?" Oscar said. "The first time I came up here I just sat and stared at it for hours. The best part is coming soon though. Just sit quietly."

Maximilian did as he was told. He didn't want to talk. He just wanted to look out at the city. He had lived his entire life in one room and now here he was, sitting on the top of a building watching the whole world pass by below. He stared out at the lights and wondered which ones were shining from his old room and whether he would ever get home again. It was a thought that made his heart feel heavy.

The city hummed on, its drone rising and falling. Then, above the muffled hum of the streets, Maximilian heard a single musical note, sweet and clear, cut through the night air. Another note joined in, and the two chased each other up and down the scales as if the notes were bouncing around the stars above. The music grew louder and swelled, more and more instruments joining in, till the whole sky seemed to be full of it. It was the most beautiful sound Maximilian had ever heard. He felt as if he was being lifted off the rooftop. He looked down to check that his paws were still in contact with the slates and heard Oscar laugh.

"That's how I felt the first time I heard it," the

black cat said.

Maximilian pricked up his ears, eager to absorb every note. "What is it?" he whispered. "Where are we?"

Oscar smiled. "We are at the Theatre Royal," he said. "The home, my friend, of the finest acting, the best ballet and the most exquisite music in the whole wide world. I come here every night to sit and listen or to watch the show."

"Watch?" Maximilian said, puzzled. "How?"

Oscar motioned towards the centre of the roof where there was a great glass dome, shimmering with light. Maximilian padded over to it, looked down and gasped at the sight. A great cavern of a room opened up below him, packed with society ladies and gentlemen dressed in their finest. They were seated row upon row before a gleaming stage on which dancers in sparkling costumes whirled and jumped as the music played on.

"That is the theatre itself," Oscar said, joining

him at the dome.

"Have you ever been inside?" Maximilian asked.

Oscar shook his head. "My days of being an indoor cat are long gone," he said. "Besides, this is not an establishment that welcomes cats."

Maximilian stared down at the finery beneath him and had an idea. The Countess often liked to go to the theatre. She would put on her best frock and her most dazzling jewels and set off for the evening, and be gone for hours. She and Count Arlington would return after midnight, with a programme decorated with tassels and embossed with the name of the theatre. Countess Arlington would stay up drinking champagne in the drawing room while ignoring the Count's yawns. She would tell Maximilian what a wonderful time she had had and who she had seen in the glamorous boxes, and whose dresses or jewels had been inferior to hers.

Could she be down there somewhere, dressed in one of her beautiful gowns?

"I want to go inside," he said. "If we can find a way."

# CHAPTER 2
## A Cat at the Theatre

The Theatre Royal was even grander than Arlington Grove. The front facade was cream stone with no fewer than nine marble columns, up which snaked carved lilies and ivy. At the top, supported by the columns, was a great triangular frieze where statues of nymphs and shepherds played music on lutes and harps. Light poured out of the front of the building through rows of round windows, and the shadows of theatregoers could be glimpsed gliding elegantly to and fro inside. The entrance was a row of six doors with leaded glass, guarded by liveried doormen in bottle-green top hats who reminded Maximilian of the stern footmen at Arlington Grove.

Maximilian and Oscar stood in the shadows across the street. They had been waiting for the right moment for Maximilian to sneak past the doormen into the lobby, but the doors had remained firmly closed. Oscar tilted his head as if listening for something. From inside the building came a pattering sound like light rain.

"Ah," he said, "applause. We must have reached a break in the show. Some people might leave now if they have dinner invitations they simply cannot miss. Keep watch. The doors will open soon."

As if to confirm Oscar's words, one of the doors swung open and a gentleman dressed in top hat and tails stepped out, swinging a silver-tipped cane.

"Now's your chance, if you're sure about

this?" Oscar said.

"I am," said Maximilian, his eyes fixed on the door.

"I shall leave you then, and wish you good luck with your adventure," said Oscar. Really, he did have the most *perfect* manners. "I'm often on the roof, if you want to come and say hello. It's been a delight to meet a cat with such good taste." And he padded off into the night, a sleek shadow mingling with the others in the street.

Maximilian watched him leave, then when one doorman was distracted by a woman in a long mink cloak asking him to call her a cab, he bounded up the steps, slipped through the open door and passed into the lobby.

The sight made his whiskers curl. The lobby was packed with society ladies in tasselled evening gowns, and gentlemen in evening suits. The beautiful music had been replaced with high-pitched chatter and the clink of glasses as waiters slipped easily through the crowd, trays of champagne held high. Maximilian moved forward, feeling his paws sink into the luxurious red carpet.

Ahead of him was a sweeping staircase, the long mahogany handrail shining almost as brightly as the gold fretwork on which it rested. Standing on the middle stair was a woman in a knee-length teal satin gown, a mink stole flung over one shoulder. Maximilian's fur stood on end. The Countess had a dress very much like this. He let out his "here I am and I should like to go home, please" miaow and was halfway up the stairs when the door at the top opened and a man with the bushiest moustache Maximilian had ever seen announced in a booming voice, "Ladies and gentlemen, please take your seats for the second act."

Still chattering, the crowd surged forwards and Maximilian found himself swept up the stairs, desperately avoiding being trampled underfoot as the theatregoers hurried back to their seats.

The door at the top of the stairs grew closer and closer and before he could let out a miaow of alarm he was inside the great theatre itself.

Maximilian looked around. The audience was excitedly settling itself into row upon row of claret velvet seats. Above him he could hear the shuffles and chatter of people taking their seats in three great half-circles of galleries that curved round above the stage. Everything was richly decorated with gold and lit by hundreds of lamps. Maximilian looked up to the great glass dome in the ceiling and squinted to see if he could spot the shadow of Oscar looking down on him.

The woman in the teal gown had disappeared. Had she been the Countess after all? Maximilian very much wanted her to be, but at the same time the thought made him uneasy. Surely the Countess would not be out enjoying herself when Maximilian was missing?

"Well, I shall just have to look for her," he said

to himself, and set off past the rows of seats, turning his head from side to side. As he neared the front of the theatre the lights fell dim and the audience was hushed. A single spotlight fell in the centre of the stage and a young girl stepped out of the shadows and began to sing. There was a brief patter of applause and then the audience fell silent and listened.

While the girl sang, Maximilian peered over the edge of the pit where the orchestra was playing and watched the violin bows hurrying up and down the scales. When the chorus joined in with a raucous song of their own, he padded up and down the rows of seats. While a romantic scene between the hero and heroine played out on the stage he sat in the middle of an aisle, entranced by the beautiful music and the light shimmering from the moon that hung at the back of the set.

*The moon indoors*, Maximilian thought. The theatre was a very odd world. One minute the people on the stage were outside in a park with trees waving in the breeze, then a great curtain of soft red velvet with gold edging would sweep across the stage and when it was pulled back they would be in a ballroom or a neat living room or even a boat on the sea. It was most peculiar.

In the middle of a comedy scene, when the

laughter of the audience echoed around the room, making the glass in the chandeliers rattle, Maximilian caught sight of a tiny pink nose and a pair of whiskers peeking out from the edge of the curtain that hung round the stage.

Maximilian felt his own whiskers tingle and he bounded up the stairs that led to the stage. The mouse gave out a tiny squeak and fled. In the middle of the stage one of the actors fell flat on his face and the audience roared. No one noticed the white cat slipping behind the scenery.

The side of the stage was dark and as crammed full of people as the lobby had been. Girls dressed in sparkling costumes were checking the sashes on each other's dresses or tying ribbons on their shoes. Men in overalls carried furniture high on their shoulders.

"Come *on*, Agnes, we're going to miss our cue!" hissed a small girl with large dimples, almost falling over Maximilian as she hurried towards the stage. Behind her, a taller girl with bobbed blonde hair was buttoning up the cuffs on her sleeves. As they reached the stage a change came over them. The girl called Agnes lost the slouch in her shoulders and pulled herself up straight, tucking her chin in and smiling out at the audience. The other girl's determined stride turned to a dainty step as she shimmied across the stage.

"This place is full of magic," marvelled Maximilian. He forgot all about the mouse, found a spot under a table and watched as the story on stage unfolded. There was a young girl who wanted to marry a footman, and her stern father and snobby mother who wanted her to marry a lord. Maximilian was entirely on the girl's side and when she ran off from her beautiful home to live free with the footman he wished that he could applaud as the audience did, but that's a difficult thing to do with paws. Instead, he waved his wonderful tail in the air. It was the highest compliment a cat could pay.

When the show ended, the actors walked to the front of the stage and bowed over and over again while the curtains swished in and out and the audience rose to their feet, the sound of their clapping echoing like thunder. Then the curtains closed for the last time and Maximilian was surrounded by noise and feet as the actors flooded off the stage. He shrank back and waited till all was quiet. As the last audience members left their seats, the lights were turned off, leaving the theatre lit only by the moon shining through the great glass dome above.

Maximilian yawned. It had been a long day and he decided to find somewhere comfortable to sleep. Earlier in the show the hero had been leaning on a particularly comfortable-looking sofa. *I wonder where that was carried to,* Maximilian thought.

He soon found it. It had been set down at the back of a room behind the stage that was full of furniture. Just looking at it made Maximilian feel very sleepy. It had plump velvet pillows and enormous tassels hung from each arm. It was the perfect place for a cat used to the best. Maximilian bounded over to it and jumped, ready to sink into the fluffy comfort of the pillows.

With an enormous crash the sofa collapsed flat to the floor and Maximilian landed on a hard sheet of painted wood. He looked down. All four paws were on the sofa, but it was flat and hard, a painted cut-out. Maximilian was shocked. It had certainly *looked* real when it was on stage. He licked his paw in a disgruntled sort of way and looked around. The room was full of other things that looked familiar. A grandfather clock that had stood at the side in one scene was leaning against a tree in the corner. Beside this hung the moon. Maximilian padded over to examine it more closely. It was a wooden frame with silver gauze stretched over it. A lamp was set into the base with a small candle inside.

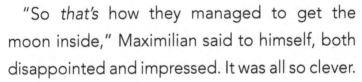

"So *that's* how they managed to get the moon inside," Maximilian said to himself, both disappointed and impressed. It was all so clever.

There was nothing to sleep on in this room so he made his way to the next and found it full of piles of fabric and costumes on rails and a huge table covered in jars of buttons and buckles.

It was also full of the most beautiful clothes he had ever seen. Maximilian was used to beautiful clothes. Countess Arlington was very fond of her dresses, especially her evening ones, the ones she called her "gowns". Maximilian was never allowed upon her lap in case he creased one of her skirts or left stray hairs on a bodice. Countess Arlington's clothes were the second most precious things in her life, after her jewellery, and every year she would have an entire new wardrobe flown into London from Paris. But, beautiful as Countess Arlington's dresses were, even *they* were nothing like as wonderful as these. There were dresses made of velvet with sleeves that dipped down to the ground, dresses with skirts made entirely of lengths of beads, shimmering in the light, and dresses with trains looped three or four times over to keep them off the floor. One dress hung on a shop dummy in the middle of the room. It seemed to be made of glass, every inch of it gleaming. As Maximilian neared it he realised that he could see his reflection in it. The dress was made of tiny mirrors, reflecting a thousand upon thousand Maximilians and bouncing light around the room.

Maximilian was just choosing which pile of fabric looked most comfortable for sleeping

when he heard a sound – a tiny, creature-like sound. He kept very still. Yes, a small grey mouse was peeking round the corner of a shoebox, checking to see if the coast was clear. It had a pompom in its mouth. *This*, thought Maximilian, *is either a tailor mouse or a thief mouse or a mouse who likes to nibble.* Whichever it was, it would be a tasty mouse.

The mouse caught sight of Maximilian, froze, and started to back off towards the shoebox. Maximilian crouched low, gathered his energy, and pounced. The shoebox skidded across the floor, mice running in all directions. They scampered up the table and catapulted

themselves across the dress rails. Some of them landed on a table that stood in the middle of the room and sent pins and rolls of cotton clattering to the floor. One landed on the mirror dress and thousands of mice suddenly appeared, reflected in its scales. Maximilian threw himself at them. He ran this way and that, and then this way again, and then that again for good measure, till he was sure that each and every mouse had been chased out of the room, squeaking indignantly.

*Chasing mice is rather good fun*, thought Maximilian. Eating them was even more fun, but sadly they had all got away. It made him think of his first mouse chase, that very morning, and how badly it had ended. If it hadn't been for that silly mouse he would still be in his comfortable window seat at Arlington Grove.

"That is a problem for tomorrow," Maximilian told himself firmly. His tummy gave a little yawn, just as his mouth gave a large one.

In one corner of the room was a pile of cushions. Maximilian curled up, tucked his wonderful fluffy tail under his chin, and closed his eyes.

Tomorrow he would find the Countess and get back home.

# CHAPTER 3
## Maximilian Gets a Job

"It's a cat, Agnes!" said the small girl with the large dimples.

"Of course it's a cat, Sylvia, I *know* a cat when I see one!" the taller girl said. "What I asked was what is it doing here?"

It was the next morning and Maximilian was sitting on his cushions. He had been found by two girls who had bustled into the room, chattering and giggling to each other. It was the two girls from the show he had seen the previous night. The tall girl was very slender, with bobbed blonde hair set in glossy waves. She had deep-blue eyes and a pretty, pouting mouth. The smaller girl's dark hair was pulled back into a neat bun. She had sparkling green eyes framed by impossibly long lashes. They were both dressed entirely in layers of net. Maximilian furrowed his brow to think where he had last seen dresses like that. Of course, it was when Countess Arlington had invited some dancers from a *corps de ballet* to entertain her guests. They had made quite a racket jumping about on the Turkish rugs, but at least they had not sung, so Maximilian had liked them.

The smaller girl, Sylvia, started to do some stretching exercises, leaning over to one side till she was almost looking at Maximilian upside down.

"Maybe Mrs Garland brought him here?" she suggested.

Mrs Garland was called for. She was a tall, thin woman with a broad, full smile. She wore a long kimono robe of scarlet silk, and her dark hair was piled up on her head and secured with one gleaming jade pin. The most remarkable thing about her was her walk. Mrs Garland walked as though she were a ship in full sail. She glided elegantly through the door, her chin held high, her feet seeming to skim across the floor under her long robe.

Sylvia stopped her little jumps and stretches when Mrs Garland was in the room and both girls stood respectfully, their hands folded neatly in front of them. Clearly

Mrs Garland was not a woman who encouraged silliness. She took one look at Maximilian, still sitting on his cushions, and clapped her hands to whisk the girls out of the room. Then she sat down on a chair and looked twinklingly at Maximilian.

"So, young man," she said, "I thought I might find you somewhere."

Maximilian's heart gave a little leap, like the ones that Sylvia had done in her pink-ribboned shoes. Countess Arlington must have come to look for him. He gave his "I'm here so there was nothing to be worried about, now can I go home?" miaow and stretched to try to catch a peek of himself in a mirror. Was he *terribly* dusty? But Countess Arlington did not come through the door looking for him. Instead, Mrs Garland held up a large velvet bag. From the bag she extracted, very carefully, an empty mousetrap. Then another. Then another, and another. Soon nineteen empty mousetraps lay on the floor in front of Maximilian. Then Mrs Garland drew from one of her pockets a pile of breadcrumbs, and from another a lump of cheese.

"And not a mouse to be seen anywhere," she declared, placing the bread and cheese on the floor. "Something, or perhaps *someone*, has kept them all away." She looked around the room. "Which means that today I am sure I will not have to sew on any pompoms or fix any nibbled hems or replace any eaten buttons." She smiled at Maximilian and from yet another pocket of her robe she drew a small package wrapped in brown paper. She unfolded it and in the middle lay a tasty-looking fresh sardine, which she placed in front of Maximilian.

Maximilian gave her his "thank you so much, I really am very hungry this morning" miaow and set to work on the sardine at once.

"Welcome to the Theatre Royal," Mrs Garland said. "I think you will have much work to do."

Maximilian had not intended to stay. When he

had finished his sardine on that first morning he had miaowed a polite "thank you so much, you have been very kind" to Mrs Garland and had set off out of the theatre to look for Countess Arlington. But the city was bigger and more confusing than he thought it would be and it did not take Maximilian long to realise that he was utterly lost. How he wished that Oscar were with him now. The black cat had known the city like the back of his paw, and Maximilian had liked his good humour and friendly nature. It was a very much more humble cat that returned to the Theatre Royal that evening. It was not home, but at least there was food and a place to sleep. He crept in through the lobby while the orchestra was tuning up for the evening show, found his way to the costume room and set to chasing away the mice.

When he awoke the next morning there was a fresh sardine waiting on a dish for him.

So Maximilian accepted the post of Theatre

Mouser, strictly on a temporary basis and to amuse himself until he could find his way home. Mrs Garland had been right about how much work there was for him! The theatre was full of mice. They nibbled the fabric of the seats and pulled out the stuffing to make their nests. They chewed through light cords, so that every night the show was in danger of being plunged into darkness. Once a whole family of them made their home inside one of the great timpani drums in the orchestra and squeaked indignantly every time the drums were struck.

Every day Maximilian would do his rounds of the theatre, chasing the mice away with a hiss and a threatening wave of his claws. Once a week he allowed himself an official day off from mousing duties and ventured out into the city on a mission to find Countess Arlington. He would walk down the streets, avoiding the kicks of passers-by and miaow his "is that you, it looks like you?" miaow at ladies who might be, but never were, her. He was not sure where Arlington Grove was, but he was sure that if he tried, he would find it one day. But after every trip he returned to the theatre more despondent and disappointed with sore feet and dusty fur.

On those days there was only one thing that could cheer him. When his work was done he would climb up to the highest corner of the gallery that hung above the stage. From there, the best seat in the house, he would watch mesmerised as the show unfolded and the wonderful tapestry of music wove its spell, soaring into the air, settling around him and smoothing back his fur. Maximilian would curl up inside his favourite songs and float away, leaving his troubles far below him.

One day, while Maximilian was watching Agnes and Sylvia powdering their faces and primping their hair ready for the performance, he had an idea.

The Pampered Pets Grooming Parlour was an exclusive establishment in one of the most elegant parts of the city. It was the grooming parlour that Countess Arlington used to take Maximilian to, regular as cuckoo-clockwork, for his weekly shampoo and hair curl. He would lie on a silk cushion for hours while cheerful girls fussed over him with combs and perfume and powder and turned him into a perfect, sweet-smelling little furball. That afternoon, between the matinee and evening performances, Maximilian made his way to the street where the grooming parlour stood.

*Perhaps someone will recognise me and tell Countess Arlington*, thought Maximilian, striding down the street towards the parlour's black-and-white striped door. He was halfway there when a very familiar car swung round the corner past him – a cream-coloured, open-topped car with leather seats and gold handles. Inside was a woman wrapped in a long fur coat. She held in her arms a fluffy white kitten with a ribbon bow around its neck that she was fussing over.

Maximilian looked at the woman and his heart gave a leap. It was Countess Arlington.

*His* Countess Arlington. With a "finally, you've found me" miaow, he sprang into action and chased the car down the street.

The car stopped outside Pampered Pets Grooming Parlour and the Countess stepped out and walked up to the door, still tickling the fluffy kitten under its chin. Maximilian leapt up the steps behind them, wound himself around Countess Arlington's feet and let out his "can I go home now, please?" miaow.

The Countess barely glanced down at him. Instead she lifted her daintily shod foot and kicked him out of the way.

"Never mind, sweetie," she said to the kitten. "Mummy won't let that nasty alley cat give you any diseases."

Maximilian reeled from the blow and stared up at her in shock.

The door of the grooming parlour opened and Countess Arlington stepped inside.

"I've brought Maximilian for his weekly

pamper," she said to the girl inside waiting to take her coat.

And the door closed on Countess Arlington and the white kitten.

Maximilian miaowed his "but I'm here" miaow and scratched at the door, but nobody opened it. He was about to miaow louder when he caught sight of himself in the gleaming polished brass letterbox of the parlour door. He saw a grubby cat with a coat full of dust from a day out in the city, not the fluffy creature that the Countess had lifted out of her car. He thought back to the last time he had seen Countess Arlington, remembering that angry look on her face as she swept out of the drawing-room door at the sight of him covered in oil and soil and dust. She had whispered something to the butler, and the butler had come back and bundled him into the cat basket.

With a start, he realised the truth. Countess Arlington had not lost him. She had abandoned him. He had made a mess and chased mice and not behaved as an Arlington cat should, and she had thrown him out. Maximilian's heart went cold. How could anyone abandon an old friend in such a way? Maximilian was a cat of many miaows, but he had no miaow for this occasion. Instead, he slunk away from the pampering parlour and back to the theatre, his heart a cold little stone, heavy in his chest.

"I've brought Maximilian for his weekly pamper," she had said.

She had even given his name away, to the kitten with the bow.

# CHAPTER 4
## A Theatre Royal Cat

Maximilian did not feel like Maximilian for the rest of that week. He moped around the costume store, barely bothering to chase the mice away and wishing that he hadn't escaped from Countess Arlington's drawing room, or chased the mice in the kitchen and made a mess, or joined in with her friends when they tried to sing around the piano. Maybe if he had behaved a little better she would still like him.

"That kitten will have my life now," he

said to Oscar. They were sitting on the dome of the roof watching Sylvia and Agnes practising down on the stage. "He even has my name."

"The kitten cannot take your name from you, Maximilian," Oscar said firmly, laying extra stress on the *Maximilian*. "As for your life, well, would you really change what you have now to be in that kitten's place?" He swept a paw round to take in the theatre below them.

Maximilian thought about this. He thought of the kitten, clutched in the Countess's hands. It would live its entire life on a comfortable cushion in the window sill of Arlington Grove. It would never chase mice or see a theatre show, or climb over rooftops or have a friend like Oscar.

He thought back to what Oscar had said that first night they sat together on the rooftops – "a cat needs space to feel alive" – and he started to feel sorry for the kitten with the bow.

Maximilian stopped waiting by the door of

the theatre to try to spot Countess Arlington. Instead of wishing he was an Arlington Grove cat he threw himself into being a Theatre Royal cat, spending his days on the roof with Oscar, in the costume store with Mrs Garland or high above the stage in the fly gallery with Bill the stage manager.

Maximilian had found the fly gallery one afternoon, after following a particularly plump mouse up a ladder. It was the place where all the wonderful scenery hung above the stage, ready to be flown down in between each scene. Maximilian liked to sit quietly tucked away in

a corner watching as Bill tied and untied the complicated knots that kept the scenery from falling down among the chorus girls' heads. Bill worked amazingly quickly, whistling to himself as the ropes flew from his hands up and down. Maximilian thought that knots looked great fun and after a while he longed to try his paw at them, but however much he miaowed his "may I have a go, please?" miaow, Bill never quite understood and would pat him on the head and offer him another sardine.

One afternoon, when the company was rehearsing a grand ballroom scene, Bill and the apprentice had just finished flying no fewer than six pieces of scenery down to the stage when the company's lunch break was called. Bill tied off the end of a rope holding a cardboard cut-out statue and hobbled over to his favourite chair. He walked with a limp, the legacy of having had a heavy stage weight fall on his toes as a young lad. He settled back and opened his lunch tin.

"Well, what have we in here today?" he said, pulling out thick slices of bread with a chunk of cheese sandwiched in the middle. He laid this on his knees and dipped into his lunch tin again. Maximilian wanted to let out his "please let there be something nice in there for me" miaow, but his manners prevented him from doing any such thing. A gentleman cat waited to see what he might be offered.

"There we go," Bill said, drawing out a small package of greaseproof paper. He unwrapped the twine and set the paper in front of Maximilian. In the middle was a slice of haddock, plump and glistening and cooked to perfection. Maximilian miaowed his "thank you so much" miaow and set to work. When he had finished the last morsel, his eye was drawn to the length of twine.

While Bill ate his lunch, leaning back contentedly in his chair and humming a cheery chorus from the theatre's Christmas show, Maximilian picked the twine up between his teeth and walked to the side of the gallery. Now was the chance to try his paw at all that knot-tying. A few days before, he had idly tried to tie a knot in his tail, but the grooming needed to make the fur lie neatly afterwards had made him decide not to repeat the experiment.

Maximilian draped the twine over a pipe that ran along the wall and tried to grasp one end with his teeth to tie it. His nose touched the edge of the twine and it fell to the floor. Maximilian sighed and tried again. It took several attempts, but eventually he had one end in his mouth and the other secured with a paw. Trying not to drop it again, he pulled the twine across and wrapped it carefully around itself twice as he had seen Bill do. With a combination of claw tweaks and nose nudges Maximilian managed to create a loop, then, with a firm pull on both ends, the knot was secure.

Maximilian flicked his tail with pride. He nudged at the knot with his nose to undo it and repeated it for practice. It was always good to turn your paw to a new skill.

While he was tying it for the third time in a row he realised that Bill was standing over him, blinking his eyes in disbelief.

"Well I never. . ." the man muttered. "I think I should go and have a lie-down. I've been overdoing things a bit lately."

Maximilian beamed. He really was a Theatre Royal cat now.

# CHAPTER 5
## Enter Madame!

One evening Maximilian was curled up under a cushion by the side of the stage failing to get a little sleep. Agnes had stayed late for a costume fitting with Mrs Garland. Sylvia was practising one of her dances on the stage, jumping up and down, criss-crossing her feet in front of one another.

"That is looking most impressive, Sylvia," called Monsieur Lavroche, the manager of the theatre, walking down through the rows of seats towards them.

Monsieur Lavroche was a tiny man with a big personality. He had short, rather spindly legs and a neat figure that was always encased in a smart dinner jacket and an array of exquisite silk waistcoats. Today he was wearing an emerald-green one, edged with white piping. A white rosebud nestled in his buttonhole.

Sylvia blushed and stopped jumping. "Thank you, Monsieur Lavroche," she said.

Monsieur Lavroche perched himself on the edge of the stage and tickled Maximilian behind the ears.

"And, Agnes," he said, "I hear that you want to be a singer?"

Agnes had a mouth full of pins and could only nod her reply. At sixteen she was a couple of years older than Sylvia, but they were the best of friends. Agnes was as lovely a singer as Sylvia was a dancer.

"She will astound us all one day," Mrs Garland said.

"Well, you will have a great example to follow this month," said Monsieur Lavroche, with a twinkle in his eye. "I wonder if you can guess who will be joining us to sing the lead role in our next show?"

He pointed knowingly to his waistcoat, but Agnes and Mrs Garland only looked at each other, puzzled, which made Monsieur Lavroche burst out laughing.

"Mrs Green, perhaps," he teased, "or Lady Olive? How about Countess Myrtle or even Madame—"

"Madame Emerald!" cried Agnes, spitting her mouthful of pins over the stage. "There was a picture of her in this week's *Society Gossip*!" Agnes jumped down from the chair that Mrs Garland had stood her on and dashed over to where she had left her bag, next to Maximilian's cushion.

"Shift over, puss," she said. Maximilian frowned. He had lived in the theatre for months and he *still* did not have a proper name from the humans. The chorus girls called him "puss", Mrs Garland called him "*mon petit chat*" and Fred, who looked after the stage door, called him "go away". Humans were ridiculously stupid sometimes. Surely he looked like a Maximilian!

"Here she is! Isn't she just beautiful?" Agnes said, holding the paper up for everyone to see. Agnes was always reading the society pages in the newspapers. She liked to cut out photos of her favourite theatre stars at society gatherings and plaster them above her dressing table, pointing out their diamond clips and ruby necklaces.

In the middle of the page was a round young woman wrapped in a voluminous satin robe. She had a sweet face with dark eyes framed by brows plucked into a high arch. There was a beauty spot above her ruby-red mouth and her lips were painted in a perfect cupid's bow shape, much like Sylvia's. Her glossy dark hair was piled up on top of her head in an elaborate coil and held in place by a sparkling diadem to match the choker at her throat. Her wrists dripped with jewels.

"Ah, but have you seen what will appear in tomorrow's edition?" Monsieur Lavroche laughed, handing a folded-up paper to Agnes. The girl snatched it eagerly and read it out to them all.

"*Madame Emerald, the great actress and skilled soprano, will spend the rest of the season with the Theatre Royal in London, playing the lead role in* The Duchess's Jewels, *a concert and ballet commissioned by the theatre for performance in front of none other than the King and Queen. Oh my!*"

Monsieur Lavroche nodded. "The King and Queen will be in the house. We have just a month to put on a splendid show for them."

"Madame Emerald! How wonderful," Agnes exclaimed. "I heard she made a wine glass shatter with one note. She sang at it till the vibrations in the air made it crack."

'She can reach a top F, you know," Sylvia added, pointing to the ceiling to indicate to Maximilian just how high that was.

Agnes pouted. "I'm sure I could sing that high too if I practised," she said primly.

Sylvia sighed. "Yes, darling, but you don't, do you," she said.

It looked as though there was going to be a quarrel, but Sylvia distracted Agnes by pointing at a circle of gems around Madame Emerald's wrist. "Look at that, Agnes," she said. "The Golden Stones. I've heard that all twelve diamonds in the bracelet were cut from a single stone and that they glow with a red and golden flame at the centre when you hold them to the setting sun. Do you think she'll wear them when she comes here?"

Agnes's eyes misted over at the thought. "The Golden Stones!" she said. "Can you think of anything more beautiful?"

She gazed again at the pretty woman in the paper and squeezed Sylvia's arm. "The great Madame Emerald, singing on stage with us!" she said. "Just imagine!"

They did not have to imagine for long. Madame Emerald arrived the very next day, accompanied by twenty-six hatboxes, nine trunks, four suitcases, five vanity cases, one large chest and a terrified maid.

Madame swept out of a carriage and up the steps to the lobby followed by harassed-looking porters staggering under the weight of her phenomenal luggage. She ignored the bow of the doorman and the nervous curtseys of Agnes and Sylvia, who had been waiting in the foyer all morning hoping for a glimpse of her, and blazed past them, her velvet cloak flying out behind her. Madame Emerald was wreathed in velvets and furs from head to foot. Her cloak

was trimmed with silver tassels and a white fur hat perched on her head. Round her throat was a mink stole.

Madame Emerald stood in the middle of the lobby while Monsieur Lavroche went through an elaborate welcome speech. She waved all his compliments aside, smiling and nodding, but not saying a word. The wide, deep red mouth that had smiled from out of the newspaper remained firmly closed.

There was something rather cartoon-like about Madame in real life, Maximilian thought. All her features seemed to have been drawn on with greasepaint, from her high arched eyebrows to the beauty spot above her lips. Maximilian stared at the beauty spot extra hard. He was sure that, in the picture in the newspaper, it had been on the opposite side. Madame's hair was not piled up on her head in the rich coils that she had worn in the paper. Instead she wore it cascading across her shoulders, hiding her full cheeks and rounded chin.

"...and so we are *most* delighted to be able to welcome you to our little theatre. Your presence will, I am sure, make the *The Duchess's Jewels* our most spectacular show yet," finished Monsieur Lavroche. He stood upright and took Madame's hand to kiss it.

Sylvia and Agnes leaned forwards. Agnes's eyes were wide and bright as she tried to catch a glimpse of Madame's wrist to see if she was wearing the famous Golden Stones.

Madame Emerald stroked her mink stole, making its tail shake as though it were alive, and gave the tiniest of bows with her head, but she said nothing.

Monsieur Lavroche assured her that she would have the most luxurious apartment they could offer her, with a suite of rooms for her exclusive use, and that absolutely nothing would be too much trouble; she only had to ask. Still Madame Emerald stayed silent.

After a while there was so much silence filling up the foyer that everyone was beginning to feel a little crowded, so Maximilian decided to do the "purr test" on Madame Emerald. He sprang to the floor, landing lightly at her feet, leaned his head against her ankle and let out a loud, rumbling *purrrrrrr.*

The great actress looked down. She opened her mouth in a great "oh" of surprise and then, throwing her arms wide so that her cloak billowed behind her, she swooped on Maximilian and gathered him to her bosom.

"Oh, I adore cats!" she cried. "He will be my special friend!"

Monsieur Lavroche stared at Madame Emerald.

Agnes's hand went to her mouth.

Sylvia's eyes widened in astonishment.

Madame Emerald had finally spoken, but instead of the dulcet tones that had charmed many an audience and society ballroom came a harsh, ratchety croak.

Was this the famous, the lovely, the celebrated Madame Emerald?

Monsieur Lavroche hesitated. "Your voice, Madame. . ." he began.

The woman froze. Maximilian thought she had the look that Bill's apprentice had when he had been caught dozing during a show or not tying off a rope properly.

"What about my voice?" she said coldly.

Monsieur Lavroche blushed. "It . . . it sounds a little . . . well . . . sore. . ." he finished.

A strange smile stole across Madame's face. "Always I am surrounded by amateurs!" she snapped. "Must a singer always be on show? Can I not be permitted to rest my voice?"

Maximilian frowned. This was rather peculiar. All of the wonderful singers that had come to the theatre before had had beautiful speaking voices as well.

"I'll show you," she croaked. "You wait! I will

67

show you all! Now, my dressing room!"

Monsieur Lavroche nodded and motioned towards the great stairwell, looking very miserable. The visit of the great Madame Emerald had not started well.

# CHAPTER 6
## A Most Peculiar Change

It was a downcast troupe that showed
Madame Emerald to her dressing room.
Clasped in her arms, Maximilian felt
himself jolted along, his head lolling
against Madame's ample bosom. She
was a very lumpy lady, he thought. It was
not a gentlemanly thing to admit, but
really she was! Being carried by her was
not at all a comfortable experience and
by the second staircase Maximilian had
had enough. Giving his "I must get back
to my duties" miaow, he tried to wriggle

out of Madame's grasp.

"*No, no*, my little cat," Madame Emerald rasped. Her voice sounded like she had been gargling with sandpaper. Maximilian wrinkled his nose and frowned at her.

"Here is your room, Madame," Monsieur Lavroche said, opening the door to the most luxurious dressing room in the theatre.

Madame Emerald nodded and smiled at him. "I am sure it will be charming," she croaked, and waved a hand at her maid.

The other woman bobbed a quick curtsey and tottered into the room. Nine hatboxes of varying sizes teetered in a great leaning tower in her hands. The porters followed her in, dropped the trunks and cases on the floor and then backed out of the room, rubbing their backs and grumbling.

"Agnes and Sylvia will help you settle in," Monsieur Lavroche began, but Madame Emerald waved him away.

"That will not be necessary," she croaked. Maximilian felt her grip on him tighten and gave a little miaow of complaint. "I have Jeanette to help me," Madame continued, stepping quickly into the room.

"Well, if you are sure, Mada—"

Jeanette, the maid, quickly closed the door on Monsieur Lavroche.

Once inside, the maid turned to Madame. The terrified expression had gone from her face and in its place was a look of triumph.

"I think that went very well, miss," she said, turning the key in the door so that no one could enter.

Madame gave a ratchety little laugh and crushed Maximilian to her.

"We're in!" she cried, her voice breaking as it rose. "What fun we are going to have!"

Madame set Maximilian down on a big armchair in the corner of the room and began to unpack her things. Maximilian thought this was very odd. Usually when a grand star visited the theatre she would laze on the velveteen chaise longue by the window or slip away across the street to the luxurious apartment reserved for the theatre's most important visitors while her maid organised the dressing room and ran errands. Maximilian had never met an actress who dealt with her own luggage.

Madame bustled around the room, unpacking box after box and exclaiming with delight over the contents, almost as though she had never seen them before. Out of Madame's trunks came dresses of such a voluminous nature that Maximilian wondered how they managed to fit into the cases at all. "We must look our best, no?" Madame tickled Maximilian on the top of his head and laughed. "Perhaps if you are good I will get a little bow tie for you too." Maximilian shuddered. Three months ago the daughter of one of the visiting ballerinas had thought it fun to dress him up and Maximilian had spent two long weeks hiding in the furniture store, terrified that she would find him and deck him with her mother's jewels and feather boas till he looked like a furry Christmas bauble.

"Oh, just look at this!" Madame cried as she drew each garment from the box.

Maximilian did not understand why she was so delighted. "Surely you've seen them all before. They are *your* dresses," he miaowed, but Madame kept taking clothes out of the boxes and squealing as if they were all new.

After the dresses came endless shoeboxes that Jeanette stacked neatly by Madame's dressing table. Then, with some difficulty, Jeanette hauled a mysterious-looking wooden box out of a trunk and heaved it on to a table by the window.

"Do you want me to put this somewhere a bit more private?" she asked Madame.

Madame glanced over at the box.

"No, that might only draw attention to it. Open

it up. If anyone asks, we can say it's for parties. After all, we'll soon have lots to celebrate."

Jeanette smiled. It was not a nice smile, Maximilian thought. It did not reach her eyes and make them twinkle like Mrs Garland's.

Jeanette turned to the box, unclipped a clasp at the front and opened it up, but from his place on the armchair Maximilian could not see what was in it.

"There we go, miss," Jeanette said. "All we need now is a couple of cocktails."

Madame laughed. Then, taking a silver key from her pocket bag, she opened the padlock on a purple satin jewel case. She drew out a deep-green necklace of jade, three tiaras, and bracelets in so many different colours that they looked like a stained-glass window. Finally she drew out a velvet parcel, placed it in front of her and unwrapped it. She held up a necklace of black and cream pearls. In the centre was the biggest diamond Maximilian had ever seen, shaped like a seven-sided star. Maximilian stared. It was very striking and, from the way she gazed at it, obviously Madame's favourite.

"Are they all there?" Jeanette asked.

Madame nodded. "All except this one."

She stretched out an arm and from the end of her sleeve peeped a bracelet of white jewels with a red flash at the centre – the Golden Stones.

"It's so pretty," she said. "No wonder she didn't want to part with it."

Maximilian miaowed his "who didn't want to part with what?" miaow.

Madame smiled at him but she did not understand. Maximilian was used to this. He could count the number of humans who could understand Cat on precisely no paws.

"I have not forgotten you, my little friend," Madame cooed. "Jeanette, find this fine cat something to eat."

Maximilian purred. He had not been disappointed in Madame. . .

Jeanette was a very different matter. Maximilian had a well-developed cat sense when it came to "people who do not, have never and are highly unlikely to ever like cats" and Jeanette was making his whiskers tingle. Every time she passed his chair she scowled down at him and remarked that "cats smell" or that "cats have been known to tear delicate costumes" or even that "cats drag mice into a place – it's unhygienic".

Jeanette and Madame could not have been more different. Madame was round and dark with fine features picked out with striking make-up that accentuated her beautiful mouth and large eyes. Jeanette, though, was a scrawny, thin-faced woman with dirty blonde hair scraped back into an untidy bun. She had very sharp cheekbones that did not quite fit with her dainty button nose, and her chin jutted out to a sharp point so that when she turned sideways she looked rather like a crescent moon.

Madame waved her objections aside. "Calm down, Jeanette," she said. "You are always so nervy. You should be more like me."

"Ooh, no, miss, you're one of a kind, you are, even if you do have a thousand faces."

Maximilian cocked his head to one side. That was an odd thing to say. Jeanette must be referring to the many parts Madame had played all over Europe.

Madame smirked at Jeanette. "Now who's taking risks?" she said, in a half-teasing sort of way. "Careful, dear. You never know who may be listening at doors." She glanced into the bag on her lap. "Ah, there it is!"

Madame drew from the bag a cut-glass bottle with a large emerald-green stopper. She opened it, sniffed it warily and winced at the smell. Maximilian had seen this before and knew what must have happened. Sylvia had been given a bottle of lavender perfume for her birthday by an elderly aunt, but by the time she opened it to use it the scent had gone off and it smelled like vinegar. Sylvia had thrown the whole bottle down the drain. But Madame did not throw the perfume down the drain. She only smiled to herself, stoppered the bottle again and placed it on a shelf on her dressing table.

Maximilian miaowed. "Shouldn't you throw that out if it smells bad?"

Madame glanced at him and yawned lazily, not even bothering to cover her mouth. It was most unladylike of her.

"I think maybe puss-cat should be put out," she said to Jeanette. "After all, we have much to prepare, don't we, dear, and he is turning out to be rather noisy."

Jeanette smirked and, picking Maximilian up without much care for where she dug in her very long nails, she slung him out of the dressing-room door and slammed it shut again.

Maximilian gave himself a little shake. He was not accustomed to such rude treatment and he was sure that Madame would scold Jeanette for her behaviour. But instead of hearing Madame tell Jeanette off, from inside Madame's dressing room he heard the two women laughing.

Maximilian had a very good nose. He could smell out a sardine buried at the bottom of a shopping basket or wrapped in several layers of greaseproof paper. What he smelled now, though, was something different. Madame claimed to be a wonderful singer, but her voice sounded like one of the harsh, yelling street-market stallholders. She claimed to love cats, but threw him out when he miaowed. She kept perfume that smelled bad, and there was something very peculiar about that beauty spot of hers. Maximilian did not need to sniff the air to smell what he was scenting now. He was scenting a mystery.

# CHAPTER 7
## The Mysterious Box

The next day the company was thrilled to hear the most beautiful singing coming from Madame Emerald's dressing room. First there were scales that started soft and low and climbed up till the topmost part of her voice echoed around the corridor outside. Then there were trills, lightly tripping up and down and ending in vibrating notes where her voice seemed to quiver with delight. She sang nonsense words that were just one vowel after another and sensible things like "Ah, fair fates" and then she sang through her solo for the finale of *The Duchess's Jewels* twice. Outside the theatre people paused in the street to listen. Downstairs, Monsieur Lavroche skipped across the lobby crying, "I knew it would be all right," and clapping his hands with delight. As he passed one of the freshly arranged flower displays at the base of the great staircase he crushed the carnation from his lapel into the pocket of his waistcoat (tangerine velvet with purple frogging) and chose a perfect cream rosebud to take its place.

Outside Madame's dressing room the company gathered, spellbound. Agnes sat cross-legged on the floor with Maximilian on her lap, gazing dreamily at Madame Emerald's door handle. Sylvia sat with her legs straight out in front of her, tapping her feet in time to the music, marking out the steps of her ballet solo.

"Isn't she wonderful?" Agnes breathed. "I told you she'd be wonderful."

"Shhh," hissed Sylvia, working out a particularly difficult step.

After half an hour the impromptu concert was over and Monsieur Lavroche whisked everyone away. He tugged on his waistcoat, straightened his collar and knocked at Madame's door.

Sylvia and Agnes hung around at the end of the corridor, hoping to catch a glimpse of Madame when she came out. Maximilian padded up to the door and pressed his ear against it. From within he heard a scratching sound and the noise of a wooden box being closed.

Then the door swung open and, as Monsieur Lavroche dropped a deep bow, coiling one hand in the air and clutching his chest with the other, Jeanette slipped into the corridor and closed the door behind her.

"Madame, so marvellous to— Oh," said Monsieur Lavroche.

"Madame is resting," Jeanette said, keeping

a firm hand on the doorknob.

"Perhaps I could just—"

"Madame is resting," Jeanette repeated.

Monsieur Lavroche was a gentleman, and a gentleman could take a hint. He tugged at his waistcoat again and coughed a rather embarrassed little cough, but he knew he was beaten. Jeanette stared at him, her face a bland mask of nothing.

"Please give her my best," he said eventually. "I look forward to seeing her at rehearsal and hearing more of her wonderful voice."

Jeanette inclined her head just a little and turned the handle.

At that moment, Sylvia and Agnes came bowling down the corridor. Ignoring Monsieur Lavroche, they made a beeline for the door to Madame's dressing room.

"We simply *must* tell Madame how much we enjoyed her singing," Agnes breathed, pushing past Jeanette and into the dressing room.

"She was splendid. I'm so glad her voice has returned," Sylvia trilled, dashing through behind her.

"Well, if everyone else is going in," miaowed Maximilian, and slipped in through Jeanette's feet.

Monsieur Lavroche frowned. It was one thing for silly girls like Sylvia and Agnes to force their way into the leading lady's dressing room, but quite another for him to do so. While he hesitated, Jeanette glared at him and, stepping back into the room, pushed the door firmly shut on Monsieur Lavroche, leaving him standing forlorn in the corridor.

Madame was stretched out on a chaise longue underneath the window, a newspaper in her hand open at the society pages. Agnes sprang towards her.

"Oh, the papers!" she cried. "Were you reading about the jewel robbery in Mayfair

six nights ago? They have photographs of all the jewels that were stolen and they are so beautiful. You must take a look, Madame. You won't believe your eyes."

Madame snatched the newspaper out of reach of Agnes's hand. Maximilian saw her eyes glance at the drawer where her own jewels were hidden. Well, that was to be expected. After all, news of a robbery would certainly make a lady nervous about her own precious pieces. He was tempted to give out his "I *told* you to lock them

away" miaow, but he did not like to appear smug.

"Jeanette, I gave strict instructions that no one—" Madame began, but Sylvia interrupted, collapsing down into one of the chairs and throwing her legs out in front of her.

"I know, but you couldn't *possibly* have meant us!" she cried. "Monsieur Lavroche is a nice old stick, but he can be *terribly* wearing, always going on about ticket sales and advertising."

"But *we're* not Monsieur Lavroche," Agnes

interjected.

"And we just wanted to hear you sing," Sylvia finished. "Goodness, is that what I think it is?"

As quickly as she had fallen into the chair, Sylvia sprang up from it and pirouetted across to the mysterious wooden box that Maximilian had puzzled over the day before. Madame sat upright on the chaise longue and moved as though to stop her, but before she or Jeanette could reach her, Sylvia had thrown open the lid of the box and clapped her hands with delight.

"Oh, it *is*! I saw one of these at a party once."

She leaned into the box and there was a crackling noise.

"Don't touch that!" Jeanette snapped, pushing her roughly aside and swiping at something inside the box. The crackling noise stopped as quickly as it had started and Jeanette slammed the box shut.

Sylvia jumped back as though she had been slapped. Maximilian saw her eyes narrow. Sylvia did not like to be ordered around, and was not about to let someone's maid treat her so rudely. She drew herself up to her full height and squared her shoulders, ready to put Jeanette firmly in her place.

Madame rose from the chaise longue and moved towards Sylvia.

"Jeanette need not have been so sharp," she said. "It's just that it's a very expensive item. It needs to be handled with care."

She turned to Jeanette. "Put something else on, Jeanette. Something we can all dance to. I would love to see Sylvia dance."

Mollified, Sylvia smiled at Madame. Maximilian saw a look pass between Jeanette and Madame. Clearly the mysterious box required further investigation. While Jeanette was busy opening it up again, Maximilian jumped up beside it and looked inside. There was a black disc with a peg in the middle, and a brass knob with a sharp needle hanging from it. Maximilian knew at once what it was now – a phonograph for playing wax records. Count Arlington had once brought one home to Arlington Grove, but the Countess would not allow it in the house and he had to get rid of it.

Jeanette took the record from the phonograph's turntable and replaced it with another. She gave the winder an extra few turns and soon the sound of an orchestra filled the little dressing room. Sylvia clapped her hands and whirled round. Madame laughed and waved her hands in the air. Agnes stepped out a merry tripping dance around the dressing table.

Only Jeanette stood, scowling, in the corner. She had the record that she had taken from the phonograph in her hand. Maximilian watched as she slipped it into a paper sleeve and tucked it behind the costumes hanging on the rail, out of sight.

# CHAPTER 8
## Goings-on and Not Goings-on

"A phonograph?" Oscar said. It was two days later and they were sitting on the roof watching some fireworks far away in the sky over Hyde Park.

Maximilian nodded. "It was most peculiar. Whatever record was on there, she didn't want anyone listening to it. I think. . ."

He paused. What he was about to say was most ungentlemanly.

"Go on," Oscar urged.

"I think there is something rather odd

about Madame."

Oscar nodded. "She does sound a little highly strung," he agreed. "That's common among singers though. The artistic temperament. I once knew a member of the Spanish Opera who would lock himself in his dressing room in the middle of the show and gargle vinegar for an hour."

Normally Maximilian loved it when Oscar told stories. His favourite ones concerned how Oscar lost his eye. Some days he would say that he lost it duelling for the honour of a beautiful Siamese cat who lived in the posh district of Mayfair. Other days he would claim that he'd been cursed by a mummy in the British Museum. This week's story was that he had stared too long at the sun, willing it to perform a total eclipse, and his eye had never recovered. Maximilian liked the duelling story best. Today, however, he was not in the mood. He had stories of his own to share.

"There's something else," he said, before Oscar could tell him any more about the strange vinegar-gargling singer. "I was in the costume store today and Mrs Garland came in in *such* a bad mood."

"That charming lady?" Oscar objected. "Impossible!"

"She has been trying to fit Madame's costumes to her but Madame will not let her *near* her. She just shouts out her measurements from behind her door. Mrs Garland is beside herself."

Maximilian bristled while he told this story. Mrs Garland was his favourite member of his theatre family. She had given him his first sardine. She had made him a cushion out of old velvet curtains. He adored her.

"Madame seems very difficult," Oscar said. "Temperamental. Did I ever tell you about the Florentine clarinet player who refused to wear purple? Fascinating fellow. He held a world record for holding his breath. . ."

But Maximilian was not listening. He gazed at the fireworks exploding in the sky above them and wondered about a different sort of record altogether. The one that Jeanette had been so keen to hide.

The next afternoon the company was gathered on the stage where Miss Julier, the theatre's musical director, was leading the chorus through a quick warm-up. They were singing very loudly to drown out the sound of the stage crew nailing together the set for the ballroom scene in *The Duchess's Jewels*. This was going to be the most expensive show the theatre had ever put on. More expensive even than the Christmas ballet with the revolving stage and the crystal coach led by six live horses.

The tenor, Archibald, who was playing the Duke, sat at the side of the stage, looking bored because no one was talking to or about him. He was tall and well built and had a taste for fancy frilled shirts and suits in rather bright colours. He had a round, genial face with a neatly trimmed goatee beard and sideburns that he would spend ages combing into place in his dressing room. His wild, curly hair was tied back at the nape of his neck with a small bow.

Archibald was terrified of something he called "the sniffles". His dressing room was full of bottles and pills that he bought from various chemists across the city, each of whom promised that they alone had the very product to protect his beautiful and precious voice. So at the time that Maximilian wandered on to the stage, Archibald was spraying his throat with a revolting concoction that smelled like pond water and making loud gargling noises up and down the scales. Madame Emerald was nowhere to be seen. Maximilian jumped lightly on to the grand piano in the orchestra pit and sat upright, tapping his claws in time to the music of the chorus.

"Wonderful, just wonderful," Miss Julier said presently, putting her baton down and smiling broadly. She was a tall woman with a beautiful smile that spread from ear to ear and then all over her face for good measure. She was taking special care over the music for the chorus and

Maximilian knew that she was giving Agnes extra singing lessons after hours at the theatre.

Miss Julier beamed at each and every member of the chorus, catching them all with her eyes.

"Monsieur Lavroche will be delighted. Now, let's run through the party scene."

She turned her lovely smile on Archibald. Maximilian thought it was utterly wasted on him. The tenor looked blankly at her, peeled himself lazily off the scenery, walked to the centre of the stage and looked towards the back of the grand auditorium, ready to sing. Archibald liked to sing. He thought it was his "duty" to let everyone hear his wonderful voice as much as they liked, and he presumed that for most people that meant "lots".

Maximilian hissed a little. He did not like Archibald.

"Shh! He'll hear you, but you're absolutely right. He's a pompous beast!"

Maximilian looked around. Perched on the

chair belonging to one of the second violins was Sylvia. Her ankle seemed to be about three times its usual size and was wrapped in sopping towels. Maximilian gave a little "miaow" of concern.

"I twisted my ankle, so I don't get to dance today," she explained, tickling him under the chin. "Stupid me. I tripped over a bag of something in the dressing-room corridor outside Madame Emerald's door. I actually saw her coming out of it while I was trying out my moving pirouette, and as I went up to talk to her, something dropped out of her dress and tripped me up. It looked like a tiny sandbag, but of course that's silly. Why on earth would Madame be carrying sandbags around?"

Maximilian frowned. Why indeed? The only place for sandbags was the fly gallery high above the theatre's stage, where Bill used them to weight the ropes.

*It would explain why she gave such lumpy*

*cuddles*, thought Maximilian, *but still. . .*

He was puzzling this interesting development when Agnes dashed over to them.

"How's the ankle, old bean? Honestly, if Madame Emerald doesn't appear, we'll be here till curtain-up on opening night!" she said.

On stage, Archibald was gathering himself in for his big song, puffing out his chest like a huge penguin and waving an arm around in circles in front of his face as though sniffing in the most divine scent on earth. Maximilian smiled. Sylvia was right. The man was very pompous indeed. He looked over to Miss Julier, who was rolling her eyes.

Archibald was about to sing when Madame swept in, her vast silk robe lifting the dust off the stage so that it burned against the footlights. Agnes jumped off the table she had been perched on and dashed forwards, eager to hear Madame's beautiful voice shown off in the wonderful acoustics of the grand theatre.

"Madame," Miss Julier cried, half bobbing her head in greeting. "Welcome to our little stage! Should we start with the party scene? Your duet with Mr Otranto?"

Madame Emerald looked over at Archibald and frowned. "If we must," she said.

Miss Julier motioned towards the pianist, who struck up the opening bars of the Duke and Duchess's duet. He had barely played two notes when Madame Emerald flung her hands to her ears.

"Stop!" she cried in alarm.

Miss Julier looked puzzled. "Stop?" she asked. "But why?"

"Oh, can you not *hear* it?" Madame exclaimed. "That pianoforte, it is an entire semitone flat! How can anyone be expected to sing to *that*?"

Miss Julier frowned. It was true that in the winter months the piano did have a tendency to go flat, but in the height of the summer it could be relied upon to keep good tone. Besides, she had tested it herself with her tuning fork that very morning.

"I think, Madame—" she began.

"You do not agree?" Madame Emerald demanded. "I cannot believe that you do not agree! Can you not hear it? What sort of musical director could not hear a flat piano! I cannot work with this."

"But, Madame—"

"And another thing," Madame continued, glaring at Miss Julier. "Where is my water? The water that I expressly said I must have with me at all rehearsals. I cannot see my water."

"Madame, we can—"

"And I do NOT like this light! This light in my eyes, it is so bright, so painful. I must have this light turned off or I do not sing. I do not sing a note."

"Bill?" called Miss Julier to the fly gallery, her voice slightly strangled. "We need to turn out—"

"And I do not have a chair!" Madame finished. "I will not stay where I am expected to stand up. This place, it is full of *amateurs*!"

And with that she swept off the stage again, like a silken whirlwind.

Miss Julier's mouth fell open in a startled little "O".

Agnes's mouth was pursed into a tiny little bow.

Archibald's mouth fell open in admiration. "What a woman!" he cried out. "That's how to behave."

And he tried to sweep out too, but tripped over a stage weight and fell on his face in the wings.

"Oh, the silly old fool," Sylvia laughed, but Maximilian was only half listening. Madame had sung so beautifully only the day before. Why would she refuse to sing now? Would she not want to show off that wonderful voice of hers? It was a puzzle, and Maximilian was beginning to rather like puzzles. Leaving Sylvia giggling over Archibald, he sprinted off after Madame.

# CHAPTER 9
## Some Puzzling Developments

Madame was very quick on her feet and she had almost reached the dressing room when Maximilian caught up with her. He managed, by a whisker, to dart in between her feet. Jeanette scowled at Maximilian and aimed a kick at him but he was too quick for her.

"Stupid animal," she snapped.

Madame slammed the door shut and leaned against it. Gone was the fury that she had shown on the stage. She wore a broad smile and her eyes were sparkling.

She began to laugh.

"Oh, Jeanette, you should have seen their faces," she giggled. "I threw the most wonderful tantrum right in the middle of that silly woman's rehearsal. She fussed and bothered about it and tried to make everything all right, but I just walked out."

She swept Maximilian up into her arms and began to step out a waltz with him around the dressing room. Maximilian was struck again by how lumpy Madame was, not soft and cuddly like Mrs Garland or angular like Agnes. Madame Emerald seemed to be made entirely of pockets and rolls of things. Being cuddled by her was most uncomfortable. Maximilian thought back to what Sylvia had said about the small bag of something that had fallen from Madame's dress. It was all most puzzling. Could Madame be hiding things under her dresses? But if that was the answer, it only lead to another question – why?

Oblivious to Maximilian's discomfort, Madame whirled around the room with him in her arms, humming softly. Then she started to sing, not one of the great pieces from *The Duchess's Jewels*, but a coarse, rude song that Maximilian had once heard one of the tradesmen's boys sing. Madame's voice was terrible. It was nothing like the gorgeous voice that they had all heard from behind her dressing-room door. It was little wonder that she had refused to sing in rehearsal, but it was still a puzzle. Why was her voice *in* the dressing room so different from the voice they had all heard that first time they listened outside it?

"And if you marry me-eeeee," she wailed. Maximilian miaowed his "pardon me, but that is not the sort of song I appreciate" miaow, but Madame ignored him.

Jeanette huffed and stamped her feet on the floor.

"And what if someone hears you?" she

snapped.

Madame stopped whirling and turned to face Jeanette. The smile left her face and she glared at Jeanette, her eyes furious. "I'll just tell them that it was you singing, *sweetie.*" She spoke the final word with a hiss and Jeanette dropped her gaze to the floor.

"I'm sorry. I just think we're taking too many risks," she said.

Madame sighed and dropped Maximilian carelessly on to a chair. Dizzy from the spinning, he almost lost his footing, which would have been most embarrassing.

Shrugging her shoulders as if she was carrying a heavy weight, Madame slipped behind a wooden screen painted with a Chinese water garden that stood at the end of the dressing room. It was in three pieces, made of exquisite lacquerwork and was there so that the leading lady could change in peace and quiet. Maximilian wondered whether he should leave.

It did not seem the act of a gentleman to be in a lady's dressing room while she was changing. He opted for looking steadfastly at the opposite end of the room, as if particularly interested in the etching of the theatre's plans that hung on the wall.

Madame stepped out from behind the screen in a pair of day pyjamas, an elegant trousers and kimono suit made of cream silk and richly embroidered with orchids and hummingbirds in pink and magenta. Maximilian gave a little jump of surprise. Where on earth had Madame (or rather, about half of Madame) *gone*? She seemed to have shrunk to a fraction of her usual size.

"That's better," she breathed. "That costume. I can't bear it. It will be a relief when this job is over and done with and I stop being Madame Emerald for good."

She ran her fingers up through her hair and gave a sharp tug. Her glossy dark locks came away, revealing golden hair tucked away in a silk net. Madame dropped the dark wig she had been wearing on the dressing-room table, removed a hairnet and shook her hair out. Blonde curls cascaded down over her shoulders.

*I* **knew** *something odd was going on here,* Maximilian thought. *Some more puzzles to solve. Why was Madame Emerald in disguise? And what did she mean by "stop being Madame Emerald?" How could anyone stop being themselves?* It was all most peculiar. Maximilian felt the fur on the tip of his tail give that telltale tingle that the mystery was deepening.

# CHAPTER 10
## Maximilian and Oscar Investigate

Maximilian stuck his head out of the skylight and miaowed his "are you there, I have news and would like some advice" miaow.

Over on the other side of the roof, Oscar stopped washing his paws and padded over.

"They're late starting," he said. "The chorus sound wonderful as always. Who is that soloist?"

"That's Agnes," said Maximilian, climbing on to the roof. "She doesn't practise enough, but she's very good."

Oscar shook his head. "Laziness," he said. "It's the curse of the talented."

He whisked his tail across the roof tiles to clear away some dust and then motioned for Maximilian to sit down. Maximilian looked a little pained at this. How Oscar could be so careless with his tail he really did not know. The thought of all that dust made Maximilian wince but Oscar did not seem to mind it one bit.

"If you're hoping to hear Madame Emerald, then you're wasting your time," Maximilian said. "She had a tantrum and refused to sing."

"Rather an odd occurrence," Oscar murmured.

"And that's not the only odd thing she's done today," Maximilian said.

He told Oscar everything that he had learned in Madame Emerald's dressing room. How she was wearing wigs, and a costume to make herself look bigger than she really was, how she couldn't wait for her time at the theatre to be over, and, most mysteriously of all, how her voice *in* the dressing room was very different from her voice *outside* it.

Oscar listened politely, nodding his head now and again and looking thoughtful. Sometimes he raised an eyebrow in surprise. Other times he tutted at Madame and Jeanette's behaviour.

"Something is most definitely going on," Maximilian said. "And I need to get to the bottom of it."

"Then I offer my services as assistant," said Oscar. "I was once assistant to a great detective in the case of the kidnapped poodle—"

Maximilian cut him short. From a window below them they heard the wonderful sound of Madame's singing, quite unlike the rough, common song that she had been wailing out in the dressing room when she whirled Maximilian around.

"She didn't sound like that five minutes ago!" Maximilian said.

Oscar looked at him thoughtfully.

"And no one else has ever *seen* her sing?" he said.

Maximilian nodded. He dashed over to where the sound was coming from and looked down at the window sill outside Madame's dressing room. It made his whiskers curl to think of what he was about to suggest. To spy on a lady was distinctly ungallant, but if he was to solve this mystery. . .

"Do you think we could get down there?" he asked.

Oscar looked at the brickwork and the criss-cross of fire escapes that hung off the building.

"Most certainly," he said. "Follow me."

A few minutes later they were hanging by their paws from an ironwork fire escape near Madame's dressing room. Maximilian was beginning to think this was a bad idea after all. What would happen if he let go?

Oscar hauled himself up and leapt easily across the window sills until he was outside Madame's window.

*How I wish I was that brave*, thought Maximilian. He tiptoed carefully to the edge of the fire escape and then jumped nervously over to join Oscar. With each leap Oscar whispered "Come on, you can do this," but Maximilian's heart was still in his mouth.

The most wonderful sound cascaded from Madame's window and people in the street below paused to listen. Maximilian and Oscar craned their heads round to look into Madame's window.

Madame was lying on a chaise longue, her head lolling back and her mouth wide open.

*What a peculiar position to sing in*, thought Maximilian.

Madame shuddered slightly and gave out a great snort. She wasn't singing at all.

"She's *snoring!*" hissed Oscar.

"So who is doing the singing?" asked Maximilian. He poked his head into the dressing room but he could see no one. The Chinese screen at the end of the room might be hiding someone, he supposed, but who?

He reached a paw inside the room.

"What are you doing?" asked Oscar.

"I'll only be a minute," Maximilian said, and jumped down into the room.

Keeping one eye on Madame, he padded over to the Chinese screen and sneaked a look round the side, but there was no one there.

*How peculiar*, thought Maximilian. He was about to investigate the costume rails in the corner of the room when he spotted a pair of boots sticking out from under them and a voice said, "Is that you, miss?"

It was Jeanette!

There was barely time for Maximilian to scoot across the room and up on to the sill before she was out from behind the rail, a plumed hat in her hand. His heart beating like an express train, Maximilian followed Oscar's lead and sped across the window sills, barely noticing how high up they were as he leapt from sill to sill. All he could think of was the new mystery. If Madame was not singing those beautiful songs, then who was?

# CHAPTER 11
## The Starburst Necklace

Maximilian had little time to puzzle over all this in the next few days. The whole theatre was abuzz with preparations for the royal performance. The chorus were called in for double rehearsals, which made them all a little tired and grumpy. Monsieur Lavroche went through an entire rainbow of waistcoats in one week and grew more and more frazzled, to the great concern of Mrs Garland. Only the doorman, Fred, was not bothered by all the activity. As long as he had his afternoon cuppa and "that 'orrible cat" kept out of his way, Fred was quite happy. Every day Monsieur Lavroche would dash down to the box office and collect the latest news of the ticket sales. Every day he became more and more excited about how everyone in London was booking to come to the royal concert.

Agnes and Sylvia were doubly excited at the prospect of dancing in front of the King and Queen. They spent a busy half-hour in between rehearsals every day practising their curtseys in front of a mirror in the dressing room.

Maximilian stepped up his efforts as Theatre Royal Mouser. The day before the performance he discovered that a family of mice had made their home under the table in the box office. It would never do if a viscount or Member of Parliament had to book their royal gala tickets while mice ran back and forth across the counter.

As he passed Monsieur Lavroche's office on his way to the lobby, Maximilian heard raised voices. He paused. He knew that it was rude to listen at doors, and he was *quite* well aware of that distasteful little saying about cats and curiosity! Still, he paused.

"She is utterly impossible!" cried Mrs Garland's voice. "I have not been able to fit a single costume to her. She has to go!"

"And I can barely get her to attend rehearsals!" Miss Julier's voice despaired. "The only times she turns up she refuses to sing. There is always some excuse or another! She is rude to the chorus and horrible to the stage crew. She has to go!"

"The show is tomorrow night and the house is packed," Monsieur Lavroche's voice said calmly. "She has to stay."

"A leading lady who won't sing! How can we even be sure that she will know what to do? Put her understudy on. Agnes. I have been training her and she knows the part inside out," Miss Julier said, her soft voice rising to a shrillness

Maximilian had not heard before.

"Perhaps we should work together," snapped Mrs Garland. "You get her to stand still to sing and I'll fit a dress round her while she's distracted."

"If you lend me one of your dressmaking pins, I could at least get her to make *some* noise," muttered Miss Julier, and Mrs Garland snorted with laughter.

"Ladies, please!" Monsieur Lavroche said. "Madame Emerald has charmed theatres and even royal palaces the world over. We know that she has learned her songs. Have we not heard them sung to us, beautifully, every note a treasure."

"And every note, so far, heard only through her dressing-room door," snapped Miss Julier.

"Madame has played every great role that there is," Monsieur Lavroche said, trying to soothe both women. "Please, do not worry. I will talk with her. I will see what I can do."

Maximilian heard mutterings from the two women but could not make out what they were saying. He leaned his head closer to the door just in time for it to open and for Mrs Garland to almost trip over him.

"What on earth are you doing there?" she chided. "I hope you're not listening at doors. Curiosity killed the. . ."

Maximilian did not stay to listen!

He went up to the dressing room to see if Agnes and Sylvia had perfected their curtseys. Agnes was playing with her make-up, drawing ice-blue swirls across her brows and accenting them with touches of glitter. They were to be fairies in the ballet sequence of the show. Sylvia, as lead dancer, had the largest wings, made from wiring and silver gauze, and Mrs Garland had given her rhinestone crystals to sew on to them. The crystals would catch the light as she danced, sending it sparkling around the theatre.

On the floor by the mirror was one of Agnes's

newspapers, open at a page of photos of a society party. At the top of the page, a beautiful girl smiled out of a picture. Her hair was cropped short in the latest style, one curl curving over her brow and held in place by a diamond and jet clip. She was dressed in a shimmering satin gown, a beaded flower at one shoulder and another on the dark sash around her hips.

She held a glass of champagne up to the camera and looked sideways at the handsome man beside her. What had made Maximilian stop and stare was her jewellery. Round her neck was a glittering necklace of black and white pearls, with a centrepiece of a large, seven-pointed star. Maximilian blinked. He was sure it was the necklace that he had seen in Madame Emerald's jewel case, the one she had held up to the light. The one that he had thought was her favourite.

Maximilian let out a loud "miaow". What on earth was Madame Emerald's necklace doing being worn by someone else?

"What's up, puss?" Agnes asked, joining him by the mirror. "Found one of those horrid mice, have you?"

She looked down at the paper and laughed. "Sylvia," she said. "Looks like puss is taken with Lady Bromley. Look, here she is at that wonderful party at the palace. Do you remember that awful story about her a few weeks ago?

That beautiful starburst necklace of hers was stolen at her house party. A lot of other jewels went missing, of course, but the necklace was the most important. A seven-pointed star on a string of black and cream pearls. She had invited about a hundred guests to her estate for the weekend and she had planned to wear the necklace to the dance on the last night. While she was dressing, someone crept into her dressing room and used knock-out drops on her. When she woke up the necklace was gone!"

Maximilian's ears pricked up as he took all this in. He was sure now that this necklace was the one in Madame Emerald's case. He remembered how she had gazed at it, that smile that was not quite nice playing over her lips. If the necklace in Madame's dressing room was really Lady Bromley's, what was Madame Emerald doing with it? He felt that familiar tingling in the tip of his tail. He knew he had to have a closer look at that necklace, and that meant getting back into Madame Emerald's dressing room.

He let out a short "you've been a great help" miaow to them both and darted out of the dressing room.

Behind him he heard Agnes laugh. "That cat! It's almost like he's talking to us!"

# CHAPTER 12
## Madame Emerald's Dressing Table

Maximilian stood on the edge of the fire escape looking down into the street far below and felt his tummy turn over. Was it only a few days ago that he had leapt across the window sills to Madame's dressing room with Oscar? How he wished that Oscar was with him now. He was not sure he had the courage to make it across on his own.

*If I fall from this height, will I land on my paws?* he wondered, then decided it would be better not to find out.

He reached a trembling paw out to the first window sill and made a small jump, landing securely on all four paws. He could feel his heart beating loudly inside him and he peered across to Madame Emerald's window. It was open but the gap was tiny. Maximilian frowned. *I hope I can squeeze through*, he thought, regretting all those double helpings of sardines.

He shuffled forwards towards the edge of the sill, ignoring his shaking legs and sticking his tail out to help his balance, and then he leapt again. His first three paws landed safely, but his back paw slipped on the shiny wood, and for a few seconds it felt as if he was going to plunge into the street below. Scrabbling wildly, he managed to regain his balance and sat, trembling and trying not to look down.

*Perhaps I could go back and find another way in*, he thought, but just as he was trying to decide whether to leap forwards towards Madame's window or back towards the fire escape his tail gave a telltale tingle. Maximilian's eyes narrowed. There was no way he was letting this mystery lie. He *had* to find out whether his suspicions about Madame were true!

He sprang forwards with greater determination and easily cleared the gap to Madame's window sill. He had been right – the window was half closed. He pressed his head through the narrow gap then, sucking in his slightly wobbly tummy and wiggling his bottom, squeezed through into Madame's dressing room.

*The first thing to do*, thought Maximilian, *is find that necklace.* If Lady Bromley's precious necklace was somewhere inside the dressing room, that would *prove* that Madame was up to no good. *It must be in her jewel box*, he thought. Maximilian remembered those nervous looks that she had cast towards the drawer with the jewel box in it when Agnes had talked about the robbery at Lady Bromley's. What if she had not been nervous for her own jewels, but because

she was hiding the stolen necklace herself?

*Well, there's only one way to find out*, he thought. In a few minutes he was by the dressing table. Madame had placed the box in the right-hand drawer, so he stood on his back paws to grasp the drawer handle between his teeth. He gave it a rough shake but it did not move. Of course, she had locked it! Maximilian shook harder. He rocked the drawer back and forth to see if he could wiggle the lock free, but it was no use. He let go of the handle and butted his head against the drawer with an annoyed miaow.

Maximilian looked around the dressing room. Really, Madame was a very messy lady. There were clothes scattered all over the chairs. He padded over to the costume rail where Madame's dresses hung and nudged one absent-mindedly with his nose. Something in it thudded to the floor, narrowly missing Maximilian's paw. It was a long cotton roll, stuffed to bursting and tied off with twine at each end.

*How odd*, he thought. He put out a paw, prodding it with his claw, and the bag split open, spilling the filling across the dressing-room floor. Maximilian sniffed it. Cotton wool and oats.

"This must have been what Sylvia saw fall from Madame's dress!" Maximilian miaowed. "But why on earth would Madame be wearing rolls of cotton wool?" He pondered for a minute or so, drumming his claws on the floor. Then all of a sudden he let out his "of course!" miaow. "She must have been stuffing her costumes to make herself look bigger!" That explained why she always looked fatter in her costumes and thinner in her day pyjamas. And it was why she gave such lumpy cuddles. *But what strange behaviour*, he thought. *Why on earth would Madame Emerald want to make herself look fatter than she really is?*

Maximilian's nose twitched. There were clues to be gathered here, even if he could not get hold of that necklace, and Maximilian was determined to sniff them out. He glanced across the room at the table near the window where the phonograph stood. He remembered there being something very odd about the way that Jeanette had spirited away that record without letting Sylvia play it. *Maybe there is a clue to be found there*, he thought, and he leapt on to the table, next to the phonograph.

It took some deft paw-work to nudge open the clasp that held the box shut tight, but eventually it swung back and Maximilian was

133

able to push the heavy lid of the box up and reveal the turntable inside.

There was a dark wax disc lying on the turntable, the brass knob with the needle resting on its edge. Maximilian stared at it. How had Madame made it turn? He nudged at the record with a paw, trying to make it spin round, but it only juddered a little and the needle made a scratching sound that set his whiskers on edge. He tried again, placing a pad of his paw on the record and pulling it towards him. This time, the wax disc spun round on the pin in the centre and a high-pitched note echoed somewhere deep in the machine.

For a third time, Maximilian pushed at the record. This time the sound echoed out of the doors at the front of the box.

"Ah, fair fates. . ." sang the record in a high, sweet voice.

Maximilian almost fell over. Surely that was Madame's voice! Not the awful, froglike one that she had used when she waltzed him around the dressing room, but the beautiful one that had stopped traffic outside the theatre and made the company set up camp outside her door in the hope of hearing a few seconds more. What on earth was she doing playing a record of her own singing in her dressing room? With a flash, he remembered his last visit to this room, when he and Oscar had sat on the window sill watching Madame snoring while someone else sang hidden away in the room.

Madame had *never* sung a note. Ever. She had pretended to sing, but all along it was the record. No wonder Jeanette had tried so hard to hide it! Maximilian had solved one mystery, but it only opened up another. Madame had been celebrated all over Europe as the finest singer ever to set foot on any stage. How could that be if she hid away in her dressing room and never sang on stage? It was impossible.

Maximilian thought about the stuffing in

Madame's clothes, and the mystery of her missing voice, and the wigs and the lies and that peculiar thing she had said about stopping "being Madame Emerald". Of course! How could he have missed the truth?

Madame Emerald was not the great, the grand, the talented Madame Emerald at all. She was an imposter. Who knew *who* she really was, or what she had done with the real Madame Emerald?

Maximilian let out a low growl. He must act at once to expose her. She could not be allowed to make a fool of all his friends. But how could he prove that she was not who she claimed to be? Maximilian looked across the room to the dressing table.

"I don't care how I do it, but I *have* to get that necklace!" he said.

He sprang to the floor and dashed over to the dressing table.

*Maybe I could hook the lock open with my*

*claw*, he thought. Last season one of the tenors had turned out to have a rather dubious past as a pickpocket, with a little lock picking on the side, and had demonstrated his skill by getting into a cabinet for which Mrs Garland had lost the key. Maximilian had been fascinated.

He jumped up on to the dressing table and dug around by the lock, squeezing the narrowest of his claws into the tiny gap between the drawer and the lock, but it was no use. The drawer remained stubbornly locked. Maximilian rattled the lock with his paw, making the whole dressing table tremble.

Behind him he heard a thud as a bottle of scent rocked on its narrow base and fell over. The cut-glass stopper rolled out and on to the floor where it smashed into a hundred tiny pieces. Maximilian chided himself. How stupid. Madame Emerald would know for sure that someone had been snooping now. He sniffed the air. He had been right about that perfume, it was definitely off. It had a harsh, sour smell, not sweet like Mrs Garland's French perfume or Agnes's fresh lavender water. He sniffed again. It was very strong too. It made him feel light-headed, almost woozy.

With the tiniest of miaows, Maximilian slumped forwards and fell in a heap to the floor.

# CHAPTER 13
## Caught and Trapped!

Maximilian woke with a mouth full of water, unable to breathe. He yelped and struggled to his feet.

In front of him stood Jeanette, glaring down at him, an upturned flower vase in one hand and a bunch of roses in the other.

"It's awake, Madame. Should I get rid of it now?" Jeanette said.

Behind her stood Madame. She had her hands clamped to her hips and a nasty, angry look on her face.

"Yes, throw it out," she snapped. "You'll have to go and buy us some more of the knock-out drops. The show is in just a few hours and we're going to need plenty of them if we're going to get those jewels."

Maximilian shrank away, shivering from the cold water and the freezing look on Madame's face. He edged towards the door, trying to think. His head felt *so* fuzzy.

"Knock-out drops" – that was what Madame had said. Agnes had mentioned them when she told Sylvia about the robbery at Lady Bromley's, and now Madame was talking openly about stealing jewels. Maximilian had no doubt now that Madame, or whoever she really was, was the thief who had attacked Lady Bromley and taken her beautiful starburst necklace. So she was dangerous too. If she should harm any of his friends. . . His fur stood on end to think of it.

Maximilian remembered what it had felt like to be out on the streets, scared and alone. Mrs

Garland, Miss Julier, Bill, Agnes and Sylvia had become his family and he wasn't about to let some horrible thief hurt them.

"Get an extra-large bottle this time, just in case," Madame muttered, pressing a roll of notes into Jeanette's hand. "And before you come back I think you should pay our *guest* a little visit. We don't want her getting away and warning the King and Queen."

"There's far too much that could go wrong," Jeanette said, buttoning up her drab coat. "We'll have that old fool Lavroche sniffing round the dressing rooms tonight."

"Oh, I can deal with him," Madame said. "We'll pop the record on a couple of times so he thinks the great Madame Emerald is in fine voice and by the time he realises the truth we'll be on a boat train to France with the Queen's jewels safely in my case along with that little trinket from Lady Bromley and the lovely stones our friend was nice enough to give me."

She held out her arm and stroked the Golden Stones bracelet on her wrist. Maximilian's head reeled. Madame was even more daring than he thought. She was planning to steal from the Queen herself!

"I suppose we have all that time when the ballet is on," said Jeanette.

Madame nodded. "Yes, they'll all be gawping at those silly girls dancing. That stupid child Sylvia will come in useful for once. Always pirouetting around the place. I would love to see her fall flat on her face."

Maximilian's fur stood on end. How dare she talk about Sylvia's lovely dancing like that! He hissed at her. Madame rounded on him, her face scowling.

"We haven't forgotten you, you little rat," she spat. "Get rid of it for good this time, Jeanette. It could ruin *everything*, miaowing and drawing attention to us all the time."

Jeanette swooped down and grabbed

Maximilian by the scruff of the neck. He let out a "how dare you, put me down at once!" yowl of anger, but Jeanette ignored him and marched along the corridor to the steps that led to the upper stairs.

Maximilian felt the jolt of every stair as Jeanette stomped up and up, through the third and fourth floors of the theatre, past the old storerooms and Bill's favourite napping spot on the top floor. He struggled and yowled, but it was no use. Everyone was downstairs making the theatre look as beautiful as possible for tonight's visitors. He was alone with Jeanette.

She carried him up through the attics, calling him a "moth-eaten old fleabag" and "interfering furball" and muttering about how she should throw him off the roof to teach him a lesson. Maximilian's heart went cold. Surely she wouldn't? When they reached the door that led to the roof she lifted him up so that she was looking him directly in the eyes.

"You'll regret you ever interfered, you little wretch!" she spat at him. "You destroyed a whole bottle of knock-out drops that we needed to use on the King and Queen tonight. Let's see if anyone finds you up here! Maybe they'll open this door in a few months' time and find a scrawny, fur-covered little skeleton!" And she threw him through the door on to the roof and slammed the door behind her.

Maximilian sprang to his feet and hurled himself at the door, but it was no use. He dashed to the skylight he usually used to get to the roof, but with no one to open it from the inside he was trapped. He crossed the roof to where the great glass dome stood over the main house and pressed his paws against the glass, looking down into the theatre, willing one of his friends to look up and see where he was. Far below him he could see Sylvia and Agnes running through their dance on the stage while Miss Julier beat time for them and clapped her hands in encouragement. Maximilian miaowed his "please notice me, I'm trapped on the roof" miaow, but no one's gaze was drawn to the small white cat high above their heads.

"What on earth are you up to?" said a voice behind him. It was Oscar, who was very surprised to find Maximilian spreadeagled across the theatre's glass dome roof.

Maximilian jumped to the ground. "Madame is a jewel thief!" he cried. "She plans to wait until everyone is watching the ballet tonight and then sneak away and steal the jewels from the Queen herself!"

"A jewel thief?" said Oscar, shocked at this latest revelation.

"She stole Lady Bromley's pearl and diamond starburst necklace. She said so to Jeanette," Maximilian said. "And goodness only knows how many other robberies she has done. Her jewel case is stuffed with tiaras and necklaces but tonight she is going to steal the Queen's jewels. We have to stop her."

Maximilian's mind flew to the beautiful rivulet of fire on Madame's wrist.

"And she has the Golden Stones!" Maximilian

said. "So she must have stolen them from Madame Emerald."

"But she *is* Madame Emerald," objected Oscar.

Maximilian shook his head. "I think she is an imposter," he said. "She cannot sing and underneath all her disguises she looks nothing like Madame Emerald. I think she must be a fake."

"Then *where*," asked Oscar, "is the real Madame Emerald?"

"She must have her hidden away somewhere," said Maximilian. "She needed her out of the way so that she could carry out her plan of stealing the Queen's jewels."

An awful thought struck him as he remembered just how terrible Madame's plan was.

"The knock-out drops! She is planning to use them on the Queen!"

Maximilian dashed to the dome and miaowed even more frantically. He tried his "quick, hurry,

Madame Emerald is a fake and has a dreadful plan" miaow and his "a terrible crime will be carried out unless you notice me" miaow and even his "there is about to be an act of treason!" miaow, but although he managed to dislodge a little dust from the inside of the dome that fluttered to the floor and made one of the maids tut, no one heard or saw him.

"It's hopeless," Maximilian said, flopping down in despair.

"The fire escape!" Oscar said. "It leads all the way down to the ground."

Maximilian dashed over to the edge of the roof and looked down. Below him the fire escape criss-crossed the building. As he was preparing to leap on to the first landing, a movement far below distracted him. A figure was emerging from the back door of the theatre – a thin woman in a dowdy coat.

Maximilian bristled. It was Jeanette. She must be going to get the knock-out drops.

STAGE DOOR

"I have to stop her somehow," he muttered. But it would take many precious minutes for a cat to make his way down all of the staircases, and Jeanette could be streets away by the time he reached the ground. It would be quicker to follow from the roof.

He looked across to the roof of the museum next door. It was a large leap and, should he fall, it was a long way down to the ground.

"I wonder where she's going..." Oscar began, but Maximilian was not listening. With a quick glance around to get his bearings, he gritted his teeth and leapt.

# CHAPTER 14
## A Rooftop Chase

Jeanette moved swiftly through the city. Maximilian shadowed her from the rooftops, keeping a close eye on her figure in the crowd as he jumped from roof to roof, swinging from guttering and dashing down fire escapes and across flagpoles. Jeanette weaved through the crowds with ease, slipping through gaps and edging round corners so that Maximilian was glad that he was high up above her, not down on the ground dodging a forest of feet and avoiding the kicks and stamps of hobnailed boots.

Still, it was hard work keeping his footing on the uneven roofs. As they headed further away from the theatre the houses became less well cared for, with loose tiles that slipped underpaw and holes that Maximilian had to leap over to avoid falling into someone's attic. At one point he thought he had lost Jeanette and, distracted, he missed his footing on a piece of wet slate. He skidded down towards the edge of the roof, his nails screaming against the tiles till he managed to catch his tail round a waterspout. Trembling a little, he scanned the road below till he saw her again, coming out of a shop and slipping a bottle into the pocket of her coat. Maximilian growled. He knew now what was in that bottle. Taking a little more care with his footing, he set off across the rooftops after her.

As Maximilian sped across the roofs he saw the streets below change. The carefully kept trees and neatly swept pavements of the grand district of the theatre disappeared, replaced by rough cobbled streets with flickering street lamps, and houses with broken windows and doors hanging off their hinges. Children near the theatre walked sedately beside nannies clad in black starched frocks, but here children in ragged frocks played noisily in the gutters, crowding round Jeanette as she walked past them and holding out their hands for pennies. Jeanette brushed them aside and strode on down the street.

Eventually Jeanette arrived at a dirty-looking house in a dirty-smelling street and knocked on the door. It was an elaborate knock, a sort of rat-a-tatter-tatter-tatter-tat-tatitty-tat sort of noise. The door opened the tiniest crack. Jeanette whispered something to the person behind it and was admitted.

Maximilian sat on the roof of a house across the street. The first task would be to get down to the ground. He looked around for a fire escape but there was no sign of one. He padded over to the side of the roof on each side, hoping that there would be an easy way down. There was a pond on one side and a tree on the other. Maximilian did not fancy seeing whether he could swim. He looked at the tree. It was tall, about a storey below him, with strong, thick branches, but still it was a larger leap than Maximilian had ever made in his life before. He looked over to the house that Jeanette had entered and squared his shoulders. He was not going to let his friends at the theatre down now.

Maximilian hunkered down and began to step from one paw to another, building up his strength and preparing to leap. He took a deep breath and pushed his paws down into the hard rooftop to put enough spring in his legs to give him the best possible jump.

Then he jumped.

And he was falling. Maximilian held his breath, his eyes widening. He was just about to cry out with a "what have I done!" miaow when his front paws slapped against one of the boughs of the tree. He mewed at the sting but his back paws sprang into life, scrabbling and catching out to steady him. He slipped through branch after branch, desperately trying to stop himself falling, and then he caught hold of the edge of a bough. He hung there by one paw, breathing a sigh of relief. Hauling himself up on to the bough, Maximilian edged his way down through the tree to the ground and dashed across the street, making a beeline for an outhouse by the side of the building.

The brickwork looked rough, with plenty of paw-holds. Maximilian's feet were sore from the fall through the tree, but still he scaled it with ease. Oscar's words of "are you a cat or a human?" from his first night out on the rooftops rang in his head. How Oscar would laugh if he could see him now! From the top of the outhouse Maximilian could see inside the building. It was sparsely furnished, with dusty cobwebs covering the windows. It didn't look as though anyone could be living here. What was Jeanette up to?

As Maximilian was judging the distance between the edge of the roof where he was perched and the nearest window sill he heard a woman's voice cry out, followed by a great crash. Maximilian sprang across the outhouse roof and pulled himself up on to his back haunches to see into the building.

Inside a small room on the first floor two men were tying a young woman to a chair. She was struggling as they pulled her hands roughly together and she looked extremely angry. Through the cracked window, Maximilian heard her shout, "You will never get away with this! Someone will unmask your fake Madame tonight!"

The door to the room swung open with a creak and Maximilian gasped as Jeanette stepped through it. She had the bottle in her hand, pouring its contents over a large square of muslin. She pressed it against the mouth of the young woman in the chair till the woman's shoulders slumped and she collapsed forwards.

"That should keep her quiet for a few more hours!" she snapped, and with that she swept out of the room. The two men slouched out after her, closing the door behind them. The young woman in the chair appeared to be in a deep, deep sleep. Maximilian remembered how woozy the liquid had made him feel, and he was a cat. Humans were well known to be far more stupid than cats, so the effect on them would be greater.

He peered over the edge of the outhouse roof. It was a long way down, but now was not the time to be a scaredy-cat. The young lady in the chair was clearly in need of the help of a brave and resourceful cat, and a brave and resourceful cat was precisely what she now had at her disposal. Maximilian hunkered down again to build up his springiness, tensed and then leapt.

He landed a little badly, paws scrabbling at the brickwork, but he did not fall. He looked carefully at the window. It was old and broken and the wood of the frame was rotting in several places. A little weight in the right place and Maximilian thought it would easily give way. He leaned against the glass where the frame looked its worst and felt the glass move a little. He pressed himself against it still harder and with a groan the pane fell into the room, followed by Maximilian. He bounced away as the glass crashed to the floor and dashed to the corner of the room, behind the door, sure that the glass would attract the attention of the two men.

He was right! Soon footsteps were thundering up the stairs and the door flew open, almost crushing him. He flicked his tail out of the way just in time to prevent it from being caught under the wood and squeezed himself up against the wall to keep out of sight. Just for once Maximilian was glad that he was a little dusty. His white fur would stand out a mile in this grubby room.

"No one in here," said a rough male voice.

"It's just the window blown in," said his

companion, kicking some of the glass so that it scudded across the floor and smashed against the wall. "Stupid house, it's falling to bits round our ears. If she'd paid a bit more we could be doing this job in comfort."

There was muttering from the first man and then they stomped out of the room, slamming the door behind them. Another pane of glass in the window shuddered and fell out into the street.

# CHAPTER 15
## A Surprising Confrontation

Maximilian raced over to the woman in the chair and nuzzled his face against her. He could smell that strange sickly odour that he had smelled in Madame's dressing room. He hoped it would not make him feel woozy again. He had to think. What was it that had brought him round when he was sleepy? Oh yes, it was Jeanette throwing a vase of water in his face. Well, that would be a little difficult to manage with paws, but maybe he could improvise. He let out a "don't worry I'm here to save you" miaow and clambered up on to the young woman's lap.

Maximilian could see a young, round, very pretty face. She looked a lot like Madame, in fact, but softer. She had a very comfortable, cuddly sort of lap, unlike Madame's lumpy one, and her hair fell in dark curls around her face.

Maximilian placed his paws on the young lady's shoulders and lifted himself up to her cheek. With a quiet "I do apologise but this is the only way" miaow he stuck out his tongue and gave the young lady's face as big a lick as a cat could manage.

She stirred a little and murmured.

Maximilian tried again.

The young lady shook her head and blinked her eyes open. Maximilian miaowed "wake up, please, we need to get out of here", and she blinked again.

The young lady looked at Maximilian in surprise.

"Where on earth did you come from?" she said. Her voice was the softest, most beautiful thing that Maximilian had ever heard. It sounded as though she was singing to him.

Maximilian miaowed "the Theatre Royal" but of course the young lady did not understand Cat. She blinked again and took a deep breath of the cold fresh air that was blowing in through the broken window. It seemed to rouse her and she looked around the room.

"Well then, puss," she said, "unless you are any good at untying knots, I think you are stuck here with me."

"Well, of *course* I can untie a knot!" miaowed Maximilian. He hopped off the lady's lap and slipped round to the back of the chair.

*Hmm*, he thought. *A simple affair; very shoddy work. Bill would not be at all impressed.* He had it undone in seconds and sprang back in front of the young lady. She did not look the type to have sardines in her pockets, but you never knew. Maximilian cocked his head to one side hopefully.

"How on earth. . ." she began. Then she laughed softly. "Well, you're a wonder, that you are," she said, and leaning forwards she offered him her hand.

"I shall call you puss," she said, "and you can

call me Madame Emerald."

Maximilian gazed at her. He had known that the woman at the theatre was a fake, and now here was the *real* Madame Emerald, sitting in front of him, with her beautiful face and her comfortable lap and her lovely, lovely voice.

The real Madame Emerald rubbed her wrists where the rope had chafed them. She stood up, walked over to the window and looked out.

"It is a long way down, puss, but I believe we can make it," she said. She put a hand to her head and breathed in again. "I just wish I didn't feel so woozy, but I'm sure I'll manage. I have five brothers, you know. I learned how to climb a tree when I was three."

Maximilian marvelled at her. Most society ladies he had seen were too scared of breaking a fingernail to even open a window, let alone climb out of one. Madame perched on the window sill and swung herself outwards. Maximilian gasped as she disappeared from sight, and tensed, waiting for the crash as she fell helpless to the ground, but all he heard was the swish of her skirt. After a couple of moments, her face appeared at the window.

"Come on, puss, you don't want to be left with those two!" she said, and disappeared again.

Maximilian sprang to the window and looked out. Below him, the lady was artfully scaling the drainpipe that led down the building. Maximilian knew he would not be able to climb the same way as she did, but he followed the only way he knew how – with a flying leap he was back on the roof of the outhouse and from there it was an easy route to the ground where he met her.

She leaned over and tickled his head.

"And now," she said, "we put a stop to her little games, don't we? Do you have a home? I suppose I should take you with me, but I'm going to the Theatre Royal, if I can find it, and I don't suppose it is any place for a cat."

Maximilian miaowed, "But that's where I live!"

Madame stood up and tiptoed towards the road, keeping a sharp eye on the windows of the house. When she reached the road she turned and beckoned to Maximilian, then she dashed out into the street and began to run.

# CHAPTER 16
## A Race Against Time

Maximilian led Madame Emerald through the streets of the city, tugging at her dress from time to time to show her the way. When the crowds grew too great, she scooped Maximilian up to her ample bosom and carried him close to her, all the while muttering darkly about what she was going to do to "that dastardly imposter" once she caught up with her. He was beginning to put two and two together. The fake Madame Emerald must have kidnapped the real one so that she could imitate her at the theatre. That was how she got her hands on the beautiful Golden Stones and all Madame's belongings. The only thing she *couldn't* imitate was Madame's wonderful voice so she had to use a record to pretend to sing. She had carried out the daring theft of Lady Bromley's necklace and now she had her eye on the jewels of the Queen of England herself!

Maximilian thought again of the knock-out drops that Jeanette had held in her hands and what the two women meant to do to the King and Queen that very night and his heart went cold. He had been so busy dashing around the city that he had not noticed that it had been getting darker and darker. The street lights of the city were beginning to glow and at the Theatre Royal the orchestra would be tuning up for the show.

Maximilian let out a loud "oh hurry, the show will be starting and there is not a moment to lose" miaow and leapt from the lady's arms. She cried out in alarm as he was nearly crushed by a passing car, then dashed after him and raced down the street. They *had* to get to the Royal Box before the show began and the fake Madame and Jeanette had the chance to put their dastardly plan into action.

It seemed like an age before they reached the theatre. Maximilian raced through the grand lobby and leapt on to the staircase. Behind him ran the real Madame Emerald. Halfway to the top of the stairs Maximilian glanced back. Madame Emerald was not following. Instead, she was heading towards the door by the side of the cloakrooms, the one that led to Monsieur Lavroche's office.

Maximilian miaowed "Not that way" but she ignored him and strode instead towards the glass-fronted door with the cream "PRIVATE" notice hanging from a chain and put her hand on the gilt fingerplate.

Maximilian leapt in front of her and miaowed again.

"Look, puss, I don't know quite why you want me to follow you, but I need to find the manager and put a stop to that woman's little games!" she said, trying to nudge him out of the way with her toes.

Maximilian miaowed again, this time with a little less patience. It was wrong of him, but this was really no time for manners.

Madame stepped over him and pushed her way through the door. Really, she was *very* determined. With a miaow of "well, I shall just have to deal with this on my own", Maximilian turned on his tail and headed up the great sweep of stairs that led to the boxes. As he reached the upper floor he could hear the music of the ballet floating up from the stage.

Outside the Royal Box a guard lay face down on the floor. Maximilian sprinted up to him and smelled the familiar sour smell of the knock-out drops. The fake Madame must be here already. She had attacked the King and Queen's guard! Bristling with anger, Maximilian pressed a furry shoulder to the door of the Royal Box.

It did not move.

Maximilian glanced around. There were more boxes on either side, full of viscountesses and countesses and even a duchess or two. He dashed to the nearest one and pushed against the door. It swung open and he rushed through, making a countess shriek as he brushed against her legs.

Maximilian miaowed his "I am so sorry for interrupting your evening" miaow and sprang on to the balcony ledge of the box. The great

auditorium stretched out below him, the light catching the jewels of the ladies and the silken top hats of the gentlemen. Down on the stage Sylvia and Agnes were twirling with garlands of flowers held high above their heads in the fairy ballet. Sylvia's wings twinkled under the stage lights, the crystals she had sewn into the gauze sending the light bouncing around the theatre. Sylvia's smile was almost as bright as her shining wings. She pointed a dainty foot and the crowd broke into a patter of applause as she whirled across the stage *en pointe*.

Maximilian focused his attention on the Royal Box, where the King and Queen were enjoying the performance immensely. The King, a broad-shouldered man with a bushy beard and curling moustaches was leaning forwards in his chair, clapping his hands enthusiastically and looking decidedly unregal in spite of the silver stars and medals that adorned the chest of his coat. Beside him sat the Queen, sitting upright in

her chair and sedately clapping three fingers against the palm of her hand. She dripped with jewels. Her eau-de-nil silk frock was set off with a ruby sash from which three diamond stars hung on velvet ribbons. At her throat were necklace upon necklace, a large diamond pendant hanging from the lowest. Her wrists shimmered with sapphires and on top of her chocolate curls rested a diamond and pearl tiara.

Maximilian peered past the King and Queen to the shadowy back of the box. Someone else was there. He growled under his breath and hunkered down, ready to leap. The fake Madame Emerald stepped from the shadows into the light. In each hand she shook out a pad of linen and, moving with the care of a cat, leaned round the King and Queen, ready to clamp them over their faces.

"MIAOW!!!!!!" Maximilian roared, and leapt towards the Royal Box. It was a substantial leap and there was no rough guttering or tree bark to catch him this time, only smooth lacquered walnut. As he landed on the balcony his paws slipped as he tried to gain a paw-hold. He felt for the grooves of the gilded carvings, but in vain, and he found himself falling for the second time that day. Maximilian let out a "Mwrow!" of alarm, and threw his legs out, desperate for something to catch his fall. He saw the King turning towards him, his brow furrowing in shock as a small white cat appeared in front of him and then fell from sight. He saw the Queen lifting a hand to her mouth. And he saw the woman behind them, her face hard as stone as she watched him fall.

Maximilian threw out his paws and his claws snagged against something soft, breaking his fall. The lights and colour of the theatre spun around him in a dizzying whirl as he dangled in mid-air, caught on one of the scarlet velvet swags that had been hung around the Royal Box. Below him there were murmurs of surprise as people in the back rows of the stalls glanced up to see a cat hanging over their heads.

Maximilian caught his breath and flexed his claws to dig them more deeply into the velvet swag. Summoning all his strength, he writhed around, slid his front claws through the soft fabric and began to haul himself up. It was hard work, with the swag slipping beneath him and swinging alarmingly with every movement he made, but Maximilian clung on and steadily climbed up to the balcony of the box. Dragging himself over the wooden railing he sprang on to the floor and advanced towards the fake Madame Emerald. His beautiful fluffy tail was ramrod straight behind him, his fur on end and prickling with anger. The Queen gave a little cry of alarm and pulled her skirts aside as Maximilian passed her, and the fake Madame made her move.

She hurled the linen squares to the floor, kicking them to the back of the box, out of sight. Maximilian stumbled a little as the smell of the knock-out drops hit him, but he pressed on, hissing at her and gnashing his teeth. The woman pounced on him, grabbing him with both hands and lifting him high in the air. Her fingernails dug into him as she twisted him this way and that and shook him from side to side making him miaow in pain.

"You stupid animal," she snapped. "Don't worry, Your Majesties – it's an alley cat. Probably riddled with disease. I'll get rid of it for you."

Maximilian let out his "the only thing we need to get rid of is you!" miaow and, wrenching his paw free, scraped his claws down her face. She screamed, staggered backwards and let him go. Maximilian fell in a heap in front of the King, who had risen and gallantly placed himself in front of his wife to protect her from this dreadful scene.

"What on *earth* is going on?" demanded the King. "What is this cat doing in the box? And who are you, madam? We didn't hear you come in. How did you get in here? Where are my guards?"

The King's deep regal tones bounced around the auditorium, making several ladies in the dress circle glance over at the Royal Box. The King had a booming bass voice, rich and sonorous. Every word resonated, demanding to be heard. Below them on the stage one of the *corps de ballet* looked up and bumped into Sylvia, sending her headlong towards the orchestra pit.

"I *demand* to know what is going on!" the King insisted, his voice growing louder.

Distracted, the conductor of the orchestra looked round and up towards the Royal Box. One by one the orchestra stopped playing and ground to a halt, first the trombones and trumpets, who had the best view of the auditorium, then the cellos and double bass. Without them the dancers started to lose step. The leader of the orchestra, a particularly fine violinist, leaned out to tap the conductor with his bow and the violins fell apart too, causing a cacophony of squeaking till eventually they gave up. A final "parp" from the bassoon dribbled away to silence.

Up in the Royal Box, the fake Madame was clutching her face where Maximilian's claws had raked a deep wound into her cheek.

"It's clearly a dangerous animal," she spat. "Just look what it did! It should be put down. It should. . ." Her words faded as the door to the box flew open. In the doorway stood the *real* Madame Emerald. Beside her stood two of the theatre doormen and Monsieur Lavroche, red in the face and wringing his hands with worry.

"YOU!" the imposter rasped. "How did *you* get here?"

"Oh, I had a little help!" Madame said, nodding towards Maximilian. Maximilian could hear the audience murmuring at the sight of the drama playing out in the Royal Box. Several people in the grand circle above were leaning over the handrails to get a better view.

The real Madame Emerald flung out an arm and pointed at her imposter.

"This woman is a jewel thief, Your Majesty," she announced. A ripple of excitement and shock ran round the audience. "She has been impersonating me in this very theatre for the last few weeks in order to gain entry to this box tonight. She is none other than Jessie Spinel, a thief well known to Scotland Yard, and had this brave animal not come to my aid this evening, no doubt she would have been picking up quite a few trinkets at tonight's entertainment."

The Queen gasped. Her hand went to her throat where her necklaces sparkled in the light, and then to the tiara on her head, and then to her arm where diamond bracelets hung in dazzling rows. She really did not know which jewels to protect first.

Maximilian stared at Madame in admiration. She was a wonderful woman. Brave, elegant and poised. He could not wait to hear her sing.

"Well, she won't get away with it, miss. We've called the police and we'll hold her till they get here," said one of the doormen. He moved forwards, ready to take hold of the woman's wrists. Maximilian relaxed a little. She was strong but she would be no match for the theatre doormen. Maximilian had once seen just two of them carrying a grand coach for the finale of the Christmas show picking up the great silver carriage as though it were a child's toy.

In the corner of the box the fake Madame, Jessie Spinel, dashed something against the wall. There was a smash and she stood there, a shard of glass flashing in her hand. The air began to fill with the smell of the knock-out drops.

"Let me through," she hissed, brandishing the sharp edges of the smashed bottle in front of her and edging her way towards the door of the box. No one dared move.

Madame Emerald stood her ground and stared at the shard of glass. She was pulling herself upright and seemed to be gathering herself in. Her arms floated slightly away from her bodice as she breathed in, deep and low, and then started to sing one single, high note. It grew and grew, resonating around the box and swelling out into the auditorium. There were exclamations of delight from the audience as the sweet, pure tone danced around the theatre. The imposter glared at Madame Emerald and stepped forwards, flashing the glass in front of her, the jagged edges glinting. Madame Emerald sang on, her voice growing louder and louder. The audience's murmurs died away into an awestruck silence. Everyone's eyes were on the Royal Box.

Beside him on the table Maximilian heard a rattle. A lead-crystal champagne glass was quivering, tiny cracks appearing in its stem. Agnes's story about the shattered wine glass rang in his head and he looked closely at the shard of glass in the imposter's hand. It began to quiver. Madame's eyes glinted. She gave one final push with her voice and the shard of glass splintered into hundreds of pieces.

"Ow!" The woman drew back her hand with alarm and looked around wildly, glaring at Madame Emerald, at the King and Queen, and finally at Maximilian, who whisked his tail away from his ears and gazed adoringly at Madame. The King stepped forwards, clapped a firm hand on Jessie Spinel's shoulder and nodded towards the two doormen.

"I think the police will be wanting to have a word with this woman," he said.

Turning to Madame Emerald he gave a regal half-bow and added, "I think you are due on stage, Madame. We have longed to hear you sing."

# CHAPTER 17
## Finally, Maximilian

"And puss here really saved you?" Agnes was saying.

"And she was really going to drug the King and Queen?" Sylvia was saying.

"And then steal the Queen's jewels?" Miss Julier was saying.

"YES!" Madame said, laughing. "She was going to wait until the King and Queen fell asleep and then steal all their jewels while everyone was watching you lovely people dance. Then she and that maid of hers would have scarpered long before it was time for her to sing in Act Two. Silly woman, she really met her match in this little puss."

Maximilian stretched himself out on the chair in Madame's dressing room. So much had happened since the night of the show. Madame had taken to the stage in the second act and had delighted everyone with that beautiful voice of hers. She had been charming to Archibald and he had been so stunned by her that he forgot to try to drown her out with his own voice. The King had insisted on the ballet being repeated so that he could enjoy it properly this time, and had praised Sylvia and Agnes for their wonderful footwork. The evening had ended with a sea of flowers being thrown on to the stage and no one stood prouder as the national anthem was played than Maximilian, a cat who had spent most of the evening on no other lap than the Queen of England's.

"But how did she get into the box?" Agnes

asked. "Surely they would have noticed."

"Would you believe it, she drugged the guards!" Madame said. "What a cheek. Then she slipped some velvet slippers on over her shoes and crept in at the back, hiding in the shadows. No one would have seen her if it wasn't for puss here."

"And Oscar," Maximilian miaowed. It would never do if he were to take all the credit.

"One thing we never solved," Sylvia said. "Why did she sound so wonderful when she was in the dressing room if she couldn't sing a note?"

Madame Emerald frowned.

Maximilian miaowed his "I can explain that one for you" miaow and jumped down from the chair. He walked over to the table where the phonograph stood and nudged at the record on the turntable.

"Ah, fair fates. . ." sang the record.

Madame Emerald gasped. "Well, I never!"

she cried. She turned to Sylvia and Agnes. "That's one of my practice records. I listen to myself sing and it helps me work out how I can improve. There is *always* room for improvement, you know, Agnes. She must have stolen it when they broke into my house to kidnap me. They were horrid, you know. They broke so many things. *And* they took all my luggage, and all my jewels. That horrible creature had taken them for herself."

She stretched out an arm. The Golden Stones glistened on her wrist. Maximilian had thought when the fake Madame arrived that she was acting as if she had never seen her clothes before. Now he knew why – she hadn't. It was everything that Madame Emerald had packed for her visit to the theatre.

Maximilian gave a "this is all falling into place nicely" miaow. Agnes leaned forwards and tickled him on the head.

"Yes, old thing, we know that it was you who

saved Madame and solved the case really," she said.

"We should reward him," Sylvia said. "Give him a proper name. We can't go on calling him plain old puss, not now he's the hero of the Theatre Royal."

Madame Emerald eyed Maximilian carefully. "How about naming him after one of the great performers who has been here?" she suggested.

Agnes frowned. "Archibald!" she announced, half giggling.

Maximilian let out a low growl. Really, one could carry a joke too far.

"Hubert!" Sylvia said, naming an actor who had fed Maximilian tuna constantly during a comedy revue that had opened at the theatre and flopped within a fortnight. Hubert was better, but still not his name.

"Allandro, after the great Allandro?" Madame suggested.

"Antonio?"

"Giovanni?"

"Maximilian?" Sylvia threw out.

Maximilian miaowed loudly. "That's my name!"

"Who?" Agnes objected.

Maximilian miaowed again. "That really is my name!"

"Well, he's never visited us but it's the name of a singer I heard in Bath once," Sylvia admitted with a sigh. "Oh, he was wonderful."

Maximilian sprang from the chair and ran to Sylvia, miaowing and skipping in circles to get her attention.

"Well, he seems to like it, so I say Maximilian it is," Madame said firmly.

"And Max for short!" added Agnes.

Maximilian looked up at his new family. A family who did not care if he left hair on the cushions or knocked over plant pots. A family who let him climb and chase mice and be himself and loved him for it. A family who would never replace him.

Finally he had his own name back. Not "puss", or "*mon petit chat*", or "go away".

Finally, Maximilian.

That night, Madame sang again. Oh, how she sang! The audience were held rapt as the beautiful notes rose and fell, dancing around the auditorium, hiding in the folds of the curtains and leaping out as echoes to surprise them.

Up on the roof, Maximilian and Oscar watched through the vast dome roof of the theatre.

"Isn't she wonderful?" sighed Maximilian.

Oscar nodded. "Exquisite. Her voice reminds me of—" He broke off. "But no, tonight is a night for *your* stories. Tell me again about how you foiled their plot."

Maximilian laughed and told Oscar for the fourth time how he had leapt from box to box to save the Queen.

"You're a tremendously brave cat, my friend," said Oscar.

"I learned from the bravest I ever met," said Maximilian with a courteous bow. He nudged a sardine across the roof towards Oscar.

"Well, perhaps we make a good team," Oscar allowed. He made a brief bow to Maximilian. "To future adventures?" he said, winking his one good eye.

Maximilian did not hesitate. "To future adventures," he said, and together they sat and watched the show unfold below them from the finest theatre seats in London.

THE END

# CURTAIN CALL

If this were a theatre show, the people I'm about to name would run on one by one and bow while you applauded them. So please give them a huge round of applause, because this book wouldn't be here without them.

Thank you to Kirsty Stansfield at Nosy Crow, who picked Max up and brushed him down so he looked his absolute best. Thank you to Fiona Scoble for being a good friend to him too. Joanna Moult, my amazing agent, thank you for taking Max to your heart and being his champion. Massive thanks to Nicola Kinnear for her fantastic portraits of Max and all his friends.

Thank you to all my lovely friends and family, especially Mum, Liz, Seren, Rick and Pete, for always believing in me, and Debbie Moon for all her writerly advice and encouragement. Thank you to all the Prime Writers for being the best writing group in the world. Thank you to all my theatre friends for providing so much inspiration over the years, particularly Cat, who first persuaded me to join a theatre group and who was my "partner in crime" in many on-stage escapades.

Most of all, thank you to Neil, best husband and best friend in the world.

**Take a bow, everyone. You're all wonderful. xxxxx**